the dating games #2:

Blind Date

Books by Melody Carlson

Devotions for Real Life

Double Take

Just Another Girl

Anything but Normal

Never Been Kissed

Allison O'Brian on Her Own—Volume 1

Allison O'Brian on Her Own—Volume 2

A Simple Song

My Amish Boyfriend

Life at Kingston High

The Jerk Magnet

The Best Friend

The Prom Queen

The Dating Games

The Dating Games #1: First Date

the dating games #2:

Blind Date

MELODY CARLSON

a division of Baker Publishing Group
Grand Rapids, Michigan

Published by Revell
a division of Baker Publishing Group
P.O. Box 6287, Grand Rapids, MI 49516-6287
www.revellbooks.com

Printed in the United States of America

Library of Congress Cataloging-in-Publication Data
Carlson, Melody.
The Dating Games. #2 Blind date / Melody Carlson.
pages cm. — (The Dating Games ; #2)
Summary: "Five friends set up blind dates for each other—will their friendships survive the experience?"— Provided by publisher.
ISBN 978-0-8007-2128-2 (pbk.)
[1. Dating (Social customs)—Fiction. 2. Clubs—Fiction. 3. Friendship—Fiction. 4. High schools—Fiction. 5. Schools—Fiction. 6. Christian life—Fiction.] I. Title. II. Title: Blind date.
PZ7.C216637Dau 2014
[Fic]—dc23 2014000481

14 15 16 17 18 19 20 7 6 5 4 3 2 1

It wasn't that Emma Parks didn't trust Devon Fremont. Except that she just didn't. The sad part was that Emma and Devon had been "best friends since diaper days"—or so their moms both claimed. But sometimes Emma doubted this. Or maybe she just remembered things differently. Like what about the time Devon whacked Emma in the forehead with Malibu Barbie's hot-pink convertible, leaving a small scar that was still visible when Emma was upset? Or how about when Devon dared her to sample fish fertilizer and Emma had hurled all over the Fremonts' new riding lawnmower—and then had been forced to clean it up while Devon watched with a devilish sparkle in her dark brown eyes?

Although it had seemed pretty cool when Devon had transferred to Emma's high school at the beginning of the school year—and despite the fact they were both members of the DG (Dating Games club)—Emma knew she needed to watch her back where Devon was concerned. This had been driven soundly home when Emma caught Devon flirting—*blatantly flirting*—with Isaac McKinley today. Less than a week after Isaac had taken Emma to the homecoming dance. Apparently that date had meant nothing!

"I don't know why you're even surprised," Cassidy Banks said nonchalantly as she drove Emma home from school on Friday.

"I guess I'm not surprised," Emma admitted. "More like hurt."

"But you know that's who Devon is," Cassidy reminded her. "Flirting is like breathing to that girl."

"Maybe so, but she knows that I still like Isaac."

"Really?" Cassidy's tone was incredulous. "Even though you've been going on and on about how you guys are just friends?"

"We *are* friends," Emma argued.

"I know. But all week you've been acting like that's all there is to it. Just friends."

"Because I don't want to push things too fast with Isaac. I mean, we both had fun at the homecoming dance. It was a cool event. But it's not like we're boyfriend-girlfriend now. You know?" Emma bit into her lip. Was that how she really felt, or was that how she wanted her friends to think she felt? Because what if everyone knew that she really was into Isaac, but his feelings toward her were . . . well, not so much?

"My point exactly, Em. You're acting like Isaac is *just your friend*. And, well, maybe in Devon's mind that means he's fair game. You can't really blame her. Isaac is a nice guy."

"Are you kidding me?" Emma stared at Cassidy in disbelief.

"You're saying he's *not* a nice guy?"

"Of course, he's a nice guy!" Emma sputtered. "But are

you seriously defending Devon on this? You of all people would take her side over mine?"

"I'm not siding with anyone," Cassidy clarified. "Just trying to be fair."

"I remember a time—not so long ago—when you couldn't stand Devon," Emma challenged. "You were always picking on her."

"Yeah, I know." Cassidy looked slightly contrite. "I'm trying to change my ways, Em."

"Seriously?"

"Yeah." Cassidy made a sheepish grin. "We're supposed to love our enemies. Remember?"

Despite her irritation, Emma laughed.

"And I'll admit it's not easy, but I've been making progress. Baby steps, you know?"

"So . . . you think of Devon like that?" Suddenly Emma felt a tinge of pity for her childhood friend. "Like she's an enemy?"

Cassidy shrugged. "Well, as you know, Devon and I have had our moments. And it's not like I approve of everything she does—that's for sure. But she's in the DG, so we have to get along."

"Like the old saying—keep your friends close and your enemies closer?" Emma teased. "But, seriously, do you think of Devon as the enemy?" Even though Emma didn't trust Devon, she wouldn't categorize her as an enemy.

"No, I don't really think she's my enemy." Cassidy slowly shook her head as she turned onto Emma's street. "And, in case you haven't noticed, I'm trying to be a better friend to her. I think she needs some good friends."

"I know." Emma sighed. "You're right."

"I really don't get why you're so bummed over Devon flirting with Isaac." Cassidy parked in front of Emma's house. "I've seen her pull the exact same stuff with Lane, and even though I like him, I try to just take it in stride. I mean, hey, if Lane's into that . . . well, maybe it's better to step back and watch him make a great big fool of himself."

"Really?" Emma wasn't so sure. "You don't feel a little jealous?"

"Sure. But maybe it takes a girl like Devon to reveal Lane's true character." Cassidy tossed a long strand of her thick dark hair over her shoulder in a nonchalant sort of way.

"*Lane's* true character?"

"You know—if he likes being hit on by a flirt like Devon, then maybe he's just a jerk and maybe I'm better off without him. And same thing for you and Isaac. Don't you think so?"

"Maybe . . . except, what guy wouldn't enjoy being hit on by a girl like Devon? You've seen her—she hangs all over them, treats them like hotties, acts like she wants to jump—"

"Yeah, yeah, I know," Cassidy cut her off. "What I'm saying is that if Lane is into that, well, let him go for it. But you'll find me heading in the opposite direction."

Emma frowned. "Okay, I get that. But don't forget how teen guys' minds work. Pastor Barry is always reminding us of this fact. You know, the HH factor—teen guys are only—"

"Human and hormonal," Cassidy finished, and they both laughed.

Emma pointed triumphantly in the air. "But, hey, what about the DG *rules*?"

"What about them?" Cassidy drummed her fingers on the steering wheel like she was eager to end this conversation and be on her way.

"We're not supposed to steal a DG member's boyfriend, *remember*?"

"But, like you just said, Emma—Isaac is *not* your boyfriend. *Remember*?"

Emma let out a long sigh. "Yeah . . . okay . . . But do you blame me for being aggravated at Devon? I mean, a lot of the time she claims that she's my best friend. Is that how a friend treats a friend?"

Cassidy made a lopsided smile. "I think Devon still has a lot to learn about being a friend. A friend to a *girl* anyway."

"Yeah. Devon seems to have the guy thing down, but when it comes to girls she needs to go back to kindergarten." Emma grinned as she reached for her bag. "Come to think of it, she didn't even have the friend thing down in kindergarten."

"So don't let her get to you," Cassidy called as Emma got out of the car.

Emma leaned back in, peering curiously at Cass. "I'm still trying to wrap my brain around this, Cass. You being so understanding when it comes to Devon—especially when I think of how she's treated you in the past. How'd you get here from there?"

Cassidy shrugged. "I just remember how hurt and helpless she seemed last week—you know, after Jason abandoned her up at the quarry after the homecoming dance. She seemed so lost and sad, and even though she tried to cover it with anger, I could tell she was frightened. It's like I began to see her differently that night."

Emma nodded. "Yeah, I get that. And when I think about some of the stuff that's happened in her life—like her parents' messy divorce and how they both pretty much ignore her now—well, I guess I do feel kinda sorry for her too." She sighed. "Thanks for the reminder." Emma waved as she shut the car door, and as she walked up to her house she realized how much she appreciated Cassidy's friendship. Sure, they hadn't been friends for as long as Devon, but Emma knew that Cass was the kind of friend she could depend on in almost any situation. Unlike Devon.

And as she unlocked the front door, she knew that Cassidy was absolutely right. Devon did need some good friends in her life. And she definitely needed friends who were not boys!

As Emma went inside, she heard her phone chiming from inside her bag. Fishing it out, she cringed to see the display. "Speak of the Devon," she said aloud. Of course, Devon was texting her—demanding that Emma call back *ASAP*. Out of habit, Emma reached for speed-dial—but then she stopped herself, pausing as the image of Devon flashed through her mind again. Emma could still see Devon clearly. She had on that snug-fitting, low-cut shirt as she leaned into Isaac, fluttering her eyelashes as she tucked a strand of fiery auburn hair behind an ear and gazed intently into Isaac's pleasantly surprised face. In Emma's imagination Devon looked like a hungry predator—and Isaac was her unsuspecting prey.

Now Emma glanced at her own image in the mirror by the front door. Mom had placed the mirror there as a reminder that they both needed to give themselves a last-minute check before leaving the house. Running her fingers through her short, layered and highlighted hair, Emma knew that her looks had improved a lot since her recent makeover—much of it at the hand of Devon. But even so, she would never turn heads—not the way Devon did. Truthfully, Emma didn't want to do that. Being flashy might be okay for Devon, but it was not Emma's style. She looked at the phone still in her hand.

"No way," she declared as she dropped it back into her bag and tossed it onto a nearby chair. Devon would have to wait. Right now, Emma was hungry. Maybe after she'd polished off a bowl of cereal and some form of fruit she'd be in a better state of mind to respond to Devon's "urgent" text. Besides, what could be that important?

Emma took her time eating Rice Krispies, then took an apple with her to the computer, munching on it as she began to cruise the internet in search of some costume ideas. The next big DG date was planned for the masquerade ball that was only two weeks away now. This ball was the school's alternative to Halloween and, because Northwood Academy was a Christian institution, no ghoulish or evil sorts of costumes were allowed. According to the posters flanking the halls, the theme this year was literature. Everyone was supposed to come dressed as a book character.

Emma had always loved playing dress-up and creating costumes. Since she was probably on the tightest budget of everyone in the DG, she knew it was in her best interest to come prepared with some clever ideas and suggestions for tomorrow's meeting—ideas that would not cost too much.

As she scanned page after page of innovative costume ideas, printing out the ones that she thought had real merit, she completely forgot about calling Devon. Or at least that's what she told herself. However, she was fully aware that her phone, which she usually kept handy, was still in her bag, still on the chair by the door right where she'd dropped it.

She was printing out a photo of a Raggedy Ann costume when she heard the doorbell ring. Knowing that her mom wasn't around to answer it, she hurried out to see who was there.

"Why didn't you call me back?" Devon demanded as she glared at Emma through the open door. It was raining outside and Devon's hair was dripping wet, which had made it go curly wild so that she resembled a female Carrot Top. It was a look that Emma knew Devon despised and would take her a couple of hours to remedy.

"Sorry." Emma stepped back to let Devon inside. "I, uh, I kinda forgot."

"Right." Devon scowled as she peeled off her soggy jacket, giving it such a hard shake that Emma got thoroughly splattered. She tossed it onto the bench by the door, then kicked off her shoes. "I know you're avoiding me."

"No, I'm not. I just—"

"Look, I'm sorry, *okay*? I know you saw me talking to Isaac at lunchtime. I know you got jealous."

Emma blinked. "Really? You knew that?"

"Duh." With hands on her hips she glowered at Emma.

"Well, how'd you expect me to feel?" Emma asked meekly.

"Like you're still my friend," Devon declared. "You know me, Em. I like to flirt. It's just the way I'm wired. It's nothing personal."

Emma slowly nodded. She wanted to point out that sometimes it felt pretty "personal" or that maybe Isaac thought it was "personal." Instead, she kept those thoughts quiet. "So what's up, Devon? Why are you so stressed?"

"My mom!" She balled her hands into fists, shaking them in the air. "I cannot believe her! She has lost her mind!"

"What's going on?"

"Has your mom said anything about it to you?" Devon stormed over to the sofa and flopped down.

"About what?"

"About my mom and Rodney."

"Rodney?"

"My mom's new boyfriend."

"Oh." Emma tried to remember if Mom had mentioned this. "I, uh, I don't think so."

"Well, Mom and Rodney took off for Vegas this morning."

"What?" Emma sat across from Devon, trying to absorb what this meant. "Your mom ran off with her boyfriend? This Rodney dude?"

Devon nodded grimly. "Yep. They're gone. *To Vegas, baby.*"

"To get married?" Emma felt slightly lost.

Devon shrugged as she slumped down onto the sofa cushions. "I doubt it. I mean, they only met a couple weeks ago. Who knows?"

"How long will they be in Vegas?" Emma asked.

"Well, since Mom has work on Monday, I'm guessing they'll be back by then." Devon reached for a pillow, punching it as if it were responsible for her anguish. "But like I said, who knows?"

"So your mom left you home alone?"

"She wrote me a note saying that I was supposed to come over here while she's gone." Devon smirked. "She obviously didn't know that my best friend was ticked at me."

"I'm not ticked at you."

"Whatever." Devon rolled her eyes. "Apparently my mom spoke to your mom this morning—neatly arranging everything. So unless you want to throw me out, you're stuck with me until Sunday." Devon folded her arms across her chest and scowled darkly. "Although I think I'm old enough to be home on my own for a few days. In fact, I think I'll just go home. You don't want me here anyway."

"Oh, Devon." Emma knew that wasn't a good idea. "You're perfectly welcome here." She forced a stiff smile. "You know that."

"Well, I wouldn't want to get in your way."

Emma studied Devon. With her tangled curls and the way her brows were pulled tightly together with her lower lip protruding slightly, Emma flashed back to when Devon had been much younger. For some reason it reminded Emma of how crushed Devon had been when her parents divorced. Suddenly, Emma felt a strong wave of compassion—similar to what Cassidy had described. Poor Devon! Her parents split up, her dad disappeared, and now her mom had run off to Vegas with a virtual stranger, abandoning Devon for who knew how long. Devon really did seem rather lost and lonely—in need of a friend.

Emma was about to express some genuine sympathy when Devon sat up straight and broke into a slightly devilish grin. "So, Em, what can we do tonight? I don't know about you, but I feel like doing something wild and crazy. You into that? Wanna have some fun?"

Emma shook her head in disbelief. So much for empathy. Really, it sometimes seemed like Devon was her own worst enemy. Did she have to drag Emma along for the ride?

I thought the DG meeting was supposed to be tomorrow," Bryn said absently into her phone. She was headed for the kitchen to scavenge leftovers from last night. "Weren't we meeting at Costello's?"

"Yeah, that was before Devon came up with some big idea," Abby explained. "Cassidy just called and said that Devon has changed the meeting to tonight instead. And she said it's urgent."

"Urgent?" Bryn stared blankly into the well-stocked fridge. No sign of any leftovers. "Tonight?"

"Apparently it has to do with our costumes for the masquerade ball. And for some reason Devon says we need to go to the mall."

"The mall?" Bryn felt her interest escalate as she closed the fridge.

"Yeah, I figured you'd be into that," Abby teased.

"Hey, the mall works for me."

"Cassidy is already picking up Emma and Devon and she'll get us next—that is if you want to go."

"Of course, I want to go. And maybe I can grab a bite at the food court since my parents went to dinner with friends tonight—and I'm starving."

"Okay, we'll be there in about fifteen."

Bryn hung up the phone and hurried to her room to change. It wasn't that she had to dress up to go to the mall, but she sure wasn't going to traipse around in her baggy sweats. After all, of the five DG members, she was the fashionista—she had a reputation to protect. And it wasn't just because she was a member of the Dating Games club, a club that the five girlfriends had created shortly after school started. The club had actually been Devon's idea—a way to get the guys in their school interested in dating. Especially since the guys had been practically coerced into giving up dating and girls as a whole. This was something that the DG was intent upon changing.

Their club had actually made good progress by setting up dates for the recent homecoming dance. But, as they all knew, their work had only just begun. And part of their agreement as DG members was to maintain their appearances. Not that Bryn needed any encouragement in this arena. Some might call her shallow, but she didn't care, because fashion was a big part of her life.

As Bryn pulled on her most recent favorite pair of jeans, she wondered what kind of plan Devon could possibly have come up with regarding their costumes for the masquerade ball. After all, they hadn't even decided which characters they were going to dress as. Oh, everyone had ideas and there'd been lots of discussions during the last few days, but so far no one had committed.

However, they had a bigger concern than not knowing how they would dress. They still hadn't lined up their dates yet. And not just regular dates either. These had to be "blind" dates for the masquerade ball. Bryn hadn't been too keen on this idea when Devon suggested it, but the rest of the DG had jumped on board. How this feat was to be accomplished remained a mystery. And so far the DG had no practical plan in place, or even any idea which guys they'd go after. There had been some hints and good-natured teasing, but as Bryn had reminded everyone today, the dance was only two weeks off and that didn't leave much wiggle room. Their goal had been to get everything nailed down at tomorrow's meeting, but apparently tomorrow was not soon enough. That was fine by her. To be honest, Bryn didn't even know how to set up a blind date. According to her mom, a blind date meant you shouldn't know the guy you were going out with. But how was that possible in a school where they knew almost everyone?

Bryn was just brushing out her long blonde hair when she heard the sound of Cassidy's car horn in the driveway. She grabbed her purse and jotted a quick note to her parents, even though she felt certain she'd be home before they returned, then hurried outside and hopped into the backseat of Cassidy's car.

"Hey, remember the last time all five of us were in Cassidy's car?" Abby asked as Cassidy backed up.

"After the homecoming dance," Emma said from in front.

"Yeah, when we had to rescue you!" Bryn said, pointing at Devon. "What a night!"

"Don't remind me." Devon groaned. "And while we're on that nasty subject, whoever ends up setting up my blind date better not try to stick me with the likes of Jason Levine, or I will—"

"Like Jason would even go out with you again anyway." Bryn laughed.

"Like I care," Devon shot back.

"We should all agree that no one in the DG will set any member up with Jason," Cassidy said in a serious tone. "Jason Levine should be officially blackballed from all Dating Games. Don't you think?"

"Absolutely," Emma said.

"So are we already having our meeting?" Bryn asked.

"Cassidy can't take notes and drive," Emma pointed out. "We'd better wait until we get to the mall."

"Why are we going to the mall anyway?" Abby asked. "We could've just met at Costello's."

"We're going to plan our costumes," Devon explained. "And I thought the mall was a good place to do it. We might want to look at clothes or shoes or jewelry, you know, for inspiration."

"I completely agree," Bryn added. "Nothing wrong with getting some fashion inspiration."

"Maybe we'll get some inspiration for our blind dates too." Devon giggled like she'd really given this some thought. "Who knows what guys might be hanging at the mall on a rainy night—especially since the football game is clear over in Brenton. What if the perfect blind date is wandering around, just waiting for the right girl to approach him?"

Bryn grinned at Devon. "That's not a bad idea."

Before long the five girls were striding through the mall. Since several of them were hungry, they decided to start their meeting in the food court. "Besides, that's where we're most likely to see the guys," Devon pointed out. "You know they're always eating."

The girls split up to get their food, then met back at a round table right in the center of the eating area. "What's that for?" Bryn pointed to the iPad on the table as she sat down.

"Cassidy wants us all to go over the rules again," Emma explained.

"It's because of me," Devon told her with a sly smile. "Cass thinks I need a reminder."

"It's for everyone," Cassidy clarified. "Kind of like a refresher course. I'll go ahead and read them while we eat." Cassidy opened a file on the iPad and read:

Dating Game Club Rules

1. We will honor the secret membership of the DG.
2. We will be loyal to our fellow DG members.
3. We will help fellow DG members to find dates with good guys.
4. We will report back to the DG regarding our dates.
5. We will not be jealous over a fellow DG member's boyfriend.
6. We will never steal a fellow DG member's boyfriend.
7. We will abstain from sex on our DG dates.
8. We will not lie to the DG about what happens on our dates.
9. We will never let a boyfriend come between fellow DG members.
10. We will admit new DG members only by unanimous vote.

As soon as Cass set down her iPad, Devon eagerly started to explain her "big idea."

"I suppose it could've waited until tomorrow," she admitted as she picked up her slice of cheese pizza, "but it's such a fabulous idea, I couldn't wait to tell you guys."

"So tell us," Abby urged.

Devon nodded eagerly. "Okay . . . So I was in the drama department talking to Mr. Ramsay about trying out for the spring play. He hasn't announced what it's going to be yet, but I wanted him to know that I played the lead at my old school—although it wasn't a musical and I heard Northwood's spring play might be a musical and—"

"What does this have to do with—"

"Hey!" Devon shook her finger at Cassidy. "*I* was talking."

"Sorry." Cassidy looked down at the iPad where she was taking notes and, unless Bryn was mistaken, looked slightly contrite—which was unusual.

"Anyway," Devon continued, "I noticed someone pushing this rack of costumes past the stage and I went over to check them out and found the most gorgeous gown ever. The guy told me it was from a Shakespeare production from a year or two ago. And it turns out it was for Juliet—and let me tell you the dress is absolutely beautiful. It's purple velvet and magenta satin and this luscious brocade skirt—it's amazing!"

"That's the dress my sister Tara wore," Bryn exclaimed. "She played Juliet in her junior year."

"Oh, yeah, I remember," Abby said. "She made such a beautiful Juliet."

"Yeah, except for that horrid black wig that Mr. Ramsay insisted she wear."

"Well, a blonde Juliet would've been—"

"*Excuse me*," Devon said loudly. "I was trying to explain my plan."

"Go ahead," Bryn said a bit indignantly. "I only wanted to point out that my sister wore that dress *and* my grandmother sewed that dress. Just in case anyone cares to know."

"Oh." Devon nodded. "Well, it's a very nice gown and it looked well made—a lot more substantial than a lot of costumes. So anyway, I took it over to Mr. Ramsay and asked him if the drama department ever loans out costumes."

"Loans out costumes?" Bryn frowned. "You mean to just anyone?"

"Mr. Ramsay said that there was not any kind of loan policy," Devon continued. "So I asked him, what about *renting* out costumes? I mean, couldn't the drama department use a little extra money to put toward the next production or to buy new costumes? I reminded him about how we're always hearing about budget cuts and how something has got to go. So what if they rented costumes and made some money for the drama department? You know, to use for future costumes." Devon beamed at them. "And Mr. Ramsay liked my idea. In fact, he liked it so much that he agreed to let me rent the Juliet costume."

"But I thought we're supposed to go as *book* characters—isn't *Romeo and Juliet* a play?" Abby asked.

"That doesn't matter," Devon told her.

"We're supposed to dress up like *literary* characters," Cassidy explained. "Anyone from literature—well, as long as they're not evil Halloween monsters. That's the whole point, to keep kids from dressing like vampires and werewolves and witches and things."

"But all those are literary characters," Devon protested.

"Yes," Cassidy agreed. "But it's still not allowed."

For a while they argued over what defined a literary

character—finally deciding that literature could be in the form of a play or a book or a poem or a fairy tale. "Even Dr. Seuss books could be literary," Emma claimed. "Anyone want to go as the Cat in the Hat?"

"Yeah, right." Bryn pointed at Devon. "Let's get back to your idea about renting the drama department costumes. Are you saying that you decided to rent the Juliet dress for yourself?" She didn't want to admit it, but she felt more than a little cheated. If anyone went as Juliet, shouldn't it be Bryn? After all, her grandma had not only sewn the gown, she had designed it too. And just for Tara—who happened to be the same size as Bryn. But now Bryn wouldn't even get the chance to wear it. This seemed all wrong, and she was determined not to take it lying down.

Devon's nod seemed a bit smug. "Yep. I'm going as Juliet. And for only twenty bucks too. It would've cost me a lot more to get a dress that pretty. So it's settled. I'll be Juliet and I'd like to know which of you guys is going to find me my Romeo."

Suddenly they were all talking and arguing at once, and Cassidy had to slap her hand on the table to get them to slow down and take turns. "Remember, this is supposed to be a meeting," Cass declared. "One at a time, *please*."

"I don't think it's fair that Devon has run ahead like this," Bryn protested. "I thought we were in this together. We were going to meet to decide which characters we'd go as and Devon just took off—"

"Hey, I thought I was doing the whole group a favor," Devon said indignantly. "You guys can rent a costume from the drama department now—all because I thought to ask. And there are some great getups available. I checked out the storage room. There are kimonos from *The Mikado*. Fairy costumes from *A Midsummer Night's Dream*. Kilts from *Brigadoon* and—"

"Okay, okay, we get it," Bryn said in an aggravated tone. "They have costumes. Duh."

"Fine. So what are you going to dress as?" Devon pointedly asked her.

"I have absolutely no idea." Bryn glared at her.

"How about you?" Devon pointed to Emma.

"I—uh—I was thinking about Raggedy Ann."

"Raggedy Ann?" Devon made a disgusted face. "That's great if you're a five-year-old. You can't possibly be serious."

"They make Raggedy Ann costumes for grown-ups too," Emma protested. "I was thinking I could make a wig from red yarn and—"

"Fine if you want to look like you're going to a children's party," Devon declared.

"I think she'd make a cute Raggedy Ann," Cassidy argued.

As aggravated as Bryn felt toward Devon, she could sort of see her point. The DG shouldn't dress up in kiddie costumes. "I kind of agree with Devon," she said slowly. "Raggedy Ann does seem a bit juvenile, Emma."

Emma bit into her lip like she was thinking hard. "Okay, how about if I go as Emma."

"Right." Bryn rolled her eyes. "Go as yourself. That's clever."

"I mean Jane Austen's Emma. *Emma Woodhouse*." Emma turned back to Devon. "Do you think the drama department would have a costume like that? The Austen books were written in, like, the eighteenth century."

"I saw a nice selection of long gowns in there," Devon assured her. "Someone said they were from *My Fair Lady* a few years back. Lots of lace and frills and ribbons and bows."

"Oh, I don't think Emma Woodhouse would wear anything too frilly," Emma told her. "I see her in a more sensible dress."

"Well, I'm sure we can find something that would work."

"My mom has the video of *Emma*, the one with Gwyneth Paltrow in it," Cassidy told Emma. "We can watch it and get some ideas. Seems like her dresses were pretty simple. And maybe we can find you a bonnet somewhere."

"And maybe a Mr. Knightley too," Emma said a bit glumly.

"Who's Mr. Knightley?" Devon asked.

"The romantic interest for Emma," Emma explained. "Like your Romeo."

"Well, let's decide on our characters first," Bryn suggested. "Then we can figure out how to get our dates."

"Okay, what are you dressing as?" Devon asked her.

"Well . . . maybe I'll go as Daisy Buchanan," Bryn told them. She wasn't even sure if she really wanted to dress as this character. She'd seen the movie some time ago and hadn't liked it that much, but she had recently started reading the novel since it was on the required reading list for English. And for some reason Bryn could relate to Daisy. Maybe it was because they were both into money and fashion and romance. Anyway, since she couldn't very well be Juliet, maybe Daisy Buchanan would be fun.

"Who's this Daisy anyway?" Devon asked. "Sounds like a hillbilly to me." She giggled. "Like Daisy Duke or Daisy Mae?"

"Daisy Buchanan just happens to be this very classy rich girl in *The Great Gatsby*," Bryn explained in a slightly arrogant tone. "She's a gorgeous blonde—*the golden girl*—and Jay Gatsby is head over heels in love with her. I'm reading the novel right now. Yes, that's definitely who I want to be."

Already Bryn was getting ideas for a costume. The book was set in the 1920s, and if she did an online search she felt certain she could find something fabulous to wear. Something that would blow the Juliet costume right out of the water. Or so she hoped. No way did she want Devon to one-up her in this. Fashion was Bryn's thing, and no matter what it took, she intended to look absolutely stunning for this dance.

"Are you getting all this down?" Abby asked Cassidy.

"Uh-huh." Cassidy nodded. "Devon is Juliet. Emma is Emma. And Bryn is Daisy." She pointed at Abby. "How about you?"

Abby made an uneasy smile. "I kind of wanted to come as Katniss Everdeen."

"Katniss from *The Hunger Games*?" Emma asked.

Bryn tried to imagine her best friend as the character from the movie she'd seen. She wondered if the fact that Abby was African American would matter, then decided it wouldn't.

"Yeah. I really enjoyed that series," Abby told them. "I've always admired Katniss for her bravery."

"I think that's a cool idea," Cassidy said. "I loved those books too. I kind of wish I'd thought of that myself."

"So you think that'd be okay?" Abby asked eagerly. "I mean, because I want to come dressed in the hunting outfit and carry a bow and—"

"But you could do one of the fancy gowns," Bryn said eagerly. "You know, those amazing outfits that Katniss wears during the ceremonies. I didn't actually read the books, but I remember the movie. And those gowns were awesome. I think they might've even won an Oscar . . . or they should've."

"The costumes were incredible." Abby nodded as she smoothed her dark, shoulder-length straightened hair. "But

I'd really like to look like Katniss when she was hunting or actually in the games, you know? Do you guys think that'd be weird for a dance?"

"I think it's great," Cassidy assured her. "It's a *masquerade* ball. You can dress up as anything—as long as it's a literary figure."

"I think Katniss is perfect for you," Emma told her.

Bryn was trying to think of a way to discourage Abby from the hunting outfit. She really wanted her best friend to come as something glamorous so that they'd look good together. "But it's a dance," she said meekly. "Don't you want to look feminine?"

"Katniss looked feminine," Cassidy argued. "And so will Abby."

Bryn pointed at Devon. "What do you think of this?"

"Well, I guess it's okay. If that's what she really wants . . ." Devon shrugged like she didn't care.

"Then it's settled. Abby is Katniss." Cassidy typed it in.

"So what about you?" Devon asked Cassidy. "Who are you dressing like?"

Cassidy frowned. "I'm not sure."

"How about Scarlett O'Hara?" Bryn suggested. "You've already got the dark hair, and just think of the beautiful gown you could wear."

"I bet we could find a good one in the drama department for you," Devon said. "There was a pretty red satin number with—"

"No." Cassidy stuck her chin out. "I'm not a Scarlett type of girl. Actually I was thinking about Dorothy—you know, from *The Wizard of Oz*. Do you guys think that's too juvenile?"

"I think that's a great idea," Emma told her. "I love Dorothy."

"Me too," Abby agreed.

"She's not very glamorous," Bryn said with dismay. What was up with these girls? Wanting to be Raggedy Ann and Dorothy . . . or Katniss in her hunting outfit? Why didn't they want to dress up in something elegant and beautiful?

"Well, Dorothy did have those ruby slippers," Abby declared.

"And why do we have to be glamorous anyway?" Emma asked. "I don't plan to be glamorous as Emma Woodhouse."

"Well . . ." Devon sighed as she put a hand on Bryn's shoulder. "I guess it's up to you and me to provide the glamour for the DG."

"Fine, you two can be the glitzy girls," Abby teased, "and the rest of us will just have fun."

"Now, we need to talk about the blind dates," Bryn told them. "It won't do us any good to have our costumes if we don't have anyone to go with."

"How are we going to do this?" Emma asked.

"I have a plan." Cassidy tore her napkin into five sections, passing one piece to everyone. "We'll all write our names down." She wrote her own name on a piece, then handed her pen to Bryn. "Then we'll each choose a name and that's the girl you'll find a date for. That way no one knows except for the one finding the date. Make sense?"

No one argued and soon they had the five wadded-up napkin pieces in the center of the table. "Now everyone take one," Cassidy said.

"What if we get our own names?" Abby's dark brown eyes flickered with concern.

"Then we'll do it again."

They all reached for a paper and then silently read the

names. Apparently, no one got their own name. But there were some quiet giggles and exchanged glances. Bryn had picked Emma's name from the pile, and although she really liked Emma, she wasn't so sure that she would be the easiest girl to find a date for—especially since Emma had been acting like she wasn't into Isaac anymore. Although Bryn had her doubts about that. To make this even more challenging, Emma tended to be fairly quiet and shy. And despite her recent makeover, she could still be something of a wallflower.

"So we really aren't supposed to tell anyone who we got?" Bryn asked with uncertainty. She wanted to confide in Cassidy since she was good friends with Emma. Cassidy might have some ideas for guys to match up with Emma. Or she might know what was up with Emma and Isaac, since he seemed like the easiest and most obvious choice.

"I don't know," Cassidy admitted. "What do you guys think?"

"I think it'll be more fun if we all keep everything a secret until the night of the dance," Emma said.

"I agree," Abby said.

"But what about the costume thing?" Devon asked. "How will my date's costume match mine? I don't want to go as Juliet with a hobbit as my date."

"That will be the responsibility of the girl who's setting him up," Cassidy declared. "Don't you think?"

They all decided that made sense.

"And except for our agreement not to match a DG member up with Jason Levine, we can pick anyone for a blind date?" Emma asked.

"Well, I've been thinking about this," Bryn said. "Won't it be nearly impossible to set a girl up with someone she doesn't know? I mean, our school's not that big."

"Good point," Abby conceded.

"So maybe we just do what we can to keep the blind dates under wraps," Emma suggested.

"Yeah." Devon nodded. "So it's mostly about the surprise, right?"

"Right," Cassidy confirmed. "Everyone should be surprised—no matter what."

"Including the guys?" Cassidy asked.

"Ooh, that's a good question," Bryn said. "It might be cool if we didn't tell the guys who they were taking out either. We could just assure them that it is one of us five."

"I like that," Devon said eagerly. "That might make it easier to get them on board." She pointed at Bryn and giggled. "We can make them all think they're going with you."

"That's not fair," Cassidy protested.

"Yeah—what if my date's disappointed?" Emma said. "Like he got me and he wanted the beautiful Bryn instead."

Bryn laughed uneasily. "That's silly, Emma. Any guy would be glad to go out with you. Anyway, we'll make it clear that if these guys aren't into the spirit of the blind date, then they can just forget it. Okay?"

Everyone agreed, and Cassidy wrote it into the meeting notes. They kicked around a few more ideas until finally Bryn could stand it no longer. "Let's go do some window-shopping," she suggested. "I want to see if I can find some shoes that would work for Daisy."

It didn't take long before the other girls got bored with shoe shopping, and nothing at the mall was really suitable for the *Gatsby* era anyway. Besides that, it seemed like Devon only wanted to look for boys. When it was getting close to 9:00,

Cassidy announced that, since she was the driver, it was time to go home.

As Cassidy drove them home, Devon started dropping hints about her hopes for her blind date. "For whom it may concern," she said, "I will be most grateful if you'd match me up with a guy who is fit to be my Romeo."

"And I'd appreciate it if my blind date is someone my parents will approve of," Abby said uneasily. "You all know how my dad can be. Don't you dare set me up with anyone like Jason Levine."

"And I would like a guy who's a good dancer," Bryn told them. "And as you know, I do think Harris is a nice guy, but the poor guy has two left feet."

They all continued to drop hints, and by the time Bryn got out of the car, she was feeling rather hopeful. The masquerade ball and the DG blind date plan might actually turn out to be pretty fun. Well, if it didn't turn into a train wreck.

Abby would have preferred to find any of the girls—anyone besides Devon—a blind date. But it was Devon's name that she'd picked up on Friday night. She had resisted the urge to toss the paper back onto the table and grab another, but if there was some way to get out of it—or get it over with quickly—she would.

It wasn't that she disliked Devon exactly, but she just didn't get her. Devon was pretty and witty and smart. In so many ways she had everything going for her. But then she invariably said or did something that just did not make sense. Sometimes it felt as if she were on a path to self-destruction. Well, that was probably too extreme. But Devon didn't seem to take life very seriously. Once when Abby had asked her what her plans for college were, Devon had rolled her eyes and said, "Who needs college to become a star?" Abby had asked what kind of a star and Devon had just laughed. As far as Abby could tell, Devon wasn't kidding because the girl did not take her studies seriously. Sometimes it seemed that Devon didn't take anything seriously.

If Abby wasn't involved in the DG—or best friends with Bryn—she probably would've shied away from someone like Devon from the start. As it was, she barely tolerated her. And now she had to find this girl a date.

"What's troubling you, honey?" Abby's mom peered curiously at her as they loaded the dishwasher together.

"Huh?" Abby feigned a blank look as she rinsed a plate.

"You're worried about something. I can tell."

Abby shrugged. "It's nothing, Mom. Just something to do with my friends."

"Uh-huh?" Mom continued watching her. "What kind of something?"

"No big deal, Mom. Really."

"Abby, I can tell you're worried. And you know what I've told you before. When you're worried about something, I feel worried too. Tell me what's up, okay?"

Abby thought hard. She knew that the DG was meant to be a secret club. But that was so that the other kids at school didn't know about it. No one had ever said they were to keep it secret from parents. Still, Abby really didn't want to confide to her mom about it.

Mom slipped an arm around Abby's shoulders. "Okay, I can't force you to talk." She chuckled. "Not like your dad can anyway."

Now Abby felt worried. What if her mom told Dad that Abby was acting strangely tonight? That could lead to real problems. Dad was at a deacons' meeting, but Abby knew that her parents talked about everything. She could imagine her mom expressing her concerns to him later tonight.

"Mom," Abby began slowly. "I'll tell you what's bugging me if you promise not to tell Dad."

Mom's brow creased. "You want me to keep something from your father?"

"It's not like it's a big deal," Abby explained. "But you know how Dad can be—he can turn something really tiny into a great big deal."

Mom chuckled. "Well, that's true sometimes—especially when it comes to his baby girl. So how about you tell me what's up, and I'll handle it as best as I can with your father."

Abby considered this. Really, what choice did she have? To say nothing guaranteed Dad would hear about it—and so she decided to tell her mom the sweetened, condensed version. Without mentioning the DG, she quickly explained about her friends' new plan to set each other up for blind dates for the upcoming dance.

"The masquerade ball?" Mom asked with interest.

"Yeah. We thought it would be fun to have blind dates."

"What a fabulous idea." Mom's eyes lit up. "What are you going to dress up as, Abby? Do you need any help?"

Abby told her about her plan to be Katniss from *The Hunger Games*.

"Interesting . . . well, that could be elegant . . ." Mom was getting that look now, like she was imagining Abby dressed to the nines. "Katniss had some gorgeous gowns in the movie. Remember the one with the flames and—"

"But I want to dress like Katniss when she was hunting. I already have a bow and a quiver—it's still in the garage, right?" Abby remembered how she'd been into archery after reading her first book back in middle school.

"As far as I know."

"And I'll wear my hair in a side braid." Abby reached up to touch her shoulder-length hair. "Although I might need some extensions to make it look right."

"That's doable." Mom nodded. "I think you'll make a lovely Katniss."

"Even though my skin's a little darker?" Abby said in a joking tone.

"I know you can pull it off, sweetie. And I just remembered I have this old leather jacket that might be perfect for your Katniss."

"Cool."

Mom frowned. "That was what was troubling you?"

Abby shrugged. It would be so easy to pretend that was all . . . but Mom was being so sweet and supportive. "The truth is I'm worried about finding a blind date for Devon. I picked her name, but I don't know her that well. She's new at school, and she and I are so different, you know? And we're not supposed to tell our other friends who we picked so I can't really ask anyone for help." She sighed. "I guess I'm worried I might set Devon up with the wrong guy."

Mom looked relieved. "Well, the dance is only one night, Abby. It's not like they'll be getting married or anything."

Abby forced a smile. "Yeah, I know."

"Just do your best. And remember the dance is supposed to be about having fun. Don't take it too seriously." She patted Abby's back.

Now Abby wished she hadn't mentioned her concerns to her mom. It figured that she didn't get it. Why should she? It had been ages since Mom was a teenager.

"I'm so impressed with how you and your friends are doing these dances together," Mom told her as she put the last glass in the dishwasher. "Your dad and I both feel much better about you dating in groups."

Abby gave the counter a quick swipe with the dishcloth.

"Do you think you girls will plan another pre-dance dinner?" Mom poured the soap in the dishwasher and closed the door. "You could have it here if you want."

"I don't know." Abby laid the dishcloth beside the sink. "But I can check with my friends."

Mom beamed at Abby. "Now see, aren't you glad we talked? It wasn't such a big deal after all. And I don't see any reason why your dad would be concerned about any of that."

Abby nodded. She knew she wasn't being a hundred percent honest with her mom. And yet she hadn't said anything untrue either. But, really, parents couldn't expect you to tell them everything, could they?

• ● ● ● •

By Tuesday Abby was still feeling overwhelmed by her assignment to find an appropriate date for Devon. Although none of the other DG members had secured a blind date yet, she could tell they were making progress. But for some reason she felt slightly stuck. Or maybe her mom was right—maybe she was making too big of a deal about it.

On one hand, Abby was tempted to just ask the next guy who spoke to her. And why not? Because, really, no matter who she asked, she felt certain Devon would not approve. But on the other hand, she felt some weird responsibility for the guy she would rope into this. What if he turned out to be a really nice guy who couldn't stand a girl like Devon? Okay, that seemed unlikely . . . but who knew?

During AP English, Abby had her eye on Leonard Mansfield.

He was a quiet, academic guy with short, dark curly hair and sincere brown eyes. He was tallish and a little on the skinny side, but if someone set Abby up with him, she wouldn't complain. Okay, maybe Leonard was slightly nerdish, but he was sweet and genuine and, in Abby's opinion, Devon could do far worse. Especially if you considered how badly Devon's date with Jason had gone. Really, who was Devon to complain? And yet she did.

Abby tried to be subtle as she pointed out Leonard during lunch. "That's Leonard Mansfield," she nonchalantly told her friends. "I have a class with him and he's really a nice guy."

"Oh . . . ?" Bryn peered curiously at Abby. "Are you saying *you like him*?"

"More than you like Kent?" Emma asked with a surprised expression.

"I like him as a friend," Abby clarified. "But I wondered if he might make a good blind date for someone . . . uh, *someone else*."

"Ugh." Devon wrinkled her nose. "You can't be serious, Abby. One of us with *that guy*?"

"Wow, I feel sorry for whoever's name you drew," Bryn told her. "You didn't get me, did you?" She laughed. "Friends don't let friends date nerds, Abs. You should know that."

"Leonard's nice," Abby argued.

"Just the name *Leonard* gives me the creeps." Devon shuddered.

"What about Leonardo DiCaprio?" Abby protested.

"That's different. Leo is good-looking." Devon actually pointed at Leonard now. "That guy resembles a scarecrow." She turned to Cassidy. "Hey, maybe Abby got your name and she thinks Leonard would make a good scarecrow to go with your Dorothy." She laughed like this was hilarious.

"He's not so bad," Emma said, but there was some uncertainty in her voice.

"Maybe you need to get to know him better," Cassidy suggested.

"That's right," Abby declared. "You guys just don't know him well enough."

"And that is exactly how some of us would like to keep it," Devon retorted.

"That's right," Bryn told Abby.

"You mean you'd write him off just like that?" Abby pointed indignantly at Bryn. "Because you guys think he looks like a scarecrow? Isn't that a little harsh? I didn't realize you were so narrow-minded and judgmental."

"Puh-lease, tell me you're not setting me up with him," Bryn said with a horrified expression. "You wouldn't do that to your best—"

"It's a secret," Cassidy sharply reminded them. *"Remember?"*

"That's right," Devon said. "No one knows who they're going with until the night of the dance."

"And maybe we should keep any guys that we're considering for blind dates under our hats too," Emma suggested. "Otherwise we might not get anywhere with this whole thing."

"Speaking of getting anywhere, has anyone had any real luck yet?" Devon asked curiously. "I mean with a guy that any of us would actually want to go out with?"

"I talked to a guy today," Cassidy said carefully. "I think he might have possibilities."

"Well, I happen to have someone seriously interested," Bryn said a bit smugly. "At first he told me to forget it, but when I explained that it would be one of us five girls, he promised to think about it. I told him he had until tomorrow to give me his answer." She chuckled. "I made it clear that he's not the only fish in this sea."

"Good point," Devon told her. "And good job."

"It figures Bryn is going to nail down the first blind date," Cassidy said a bit dismally. "The poor guy probably thinks he's going to take her to the dance."

Bryn shrugged. "Hey, I didn't say anything to make him think that."

• • ● • •

As it turned out, Cassidy was right—Bryn was the first one to secure a blind date. Of course, no one but Bryn knew who the mystery guy was or who he was taking to the dance, but by Wednesday morning, there was one blind date down and four to go.

"And I'll bet that I'm the next one to set up a date," Devon challenged the others as they convened in the locker bay before first period.

"That's a bet I won't be taking," Emma said glumly.

"Me neither," Cassidy added. "Turns out that the guy I had in mind already asked someone else."

Devon pointed at Abby now. "How about you? Oh, I nearly forgot," she teased, "you're working on the nerdy department, aren't you?"

Abby glared at her. Why did Devon have to be so mean sometimes?

"Guess it's up to you and me then." Devon locked arms

with Bryn. "Leave it to the women to teach the little girls how it's done." Then, laughing, she led Bryn away. For some reason that really got to Abby. It was like Devon was trying to take over Bryn . . . like they were becoming best friends and pushing Abby aside. Abby knew it was silly to feel threatened like that. She knew that Bryn was only playing along. But all the same, it hurt.

Perhaps that was why Abby decided to approach Leonard in AP English—although that was not what she told herself as she watched him sit down in front of a computer. She was tired of fretting over this whole stupid blind date thing. She was also concerned that it was affecting her schoolwork, and if she didn't keep her grades up, Dad would make her pull out of the sports that she loved. She just didn't need this kind of distraction in her life.

Besides, as her mom had pointed out, it wasn't like Devon was going to have to marry the boy. Plus there was the possibility that Leonard would reject the whole thing. Because it was an independent study day, she had the freedom and opportunity to engage Leonard in a real conversation. This was her chance. Taking a deep breath, she wandered over to where Leonard was working and began to make small talk about the assignment. Leonard seemed genuinely happy to chat with her and after a couple minutes, she got up the nerve to mention the upcoming dance.

"You know we're supposed to dress up like literary characters." She pointed at the computer screen where he was reading about Edgar Allen Poe. "Poe probably has some great characters to choose from."

"That's for sure." He nodded eagerly. "You know I was on the Honor Society planning committee for the dance this year—in fact I was the one who suggested literary characters. Jessica Thistle wanted to go with characters from movies. She called it Hollywood Halloween. Thankfully that got voted down."

"Oh yeah. Right." Now Abby explained how she and her friends all wanted to go to the dance. "We've already figured out our characters and costumes and stuff."

"That's cool." He smoothed the front of his shirt. "I was thinking I'd like to go too." He made a nervous laugh. "Not that I have a girl to go with me. Not yet anyway."

"Really? So . . . what if I knew of a girl who'd like to go with you?"

His eyes lit up. "Could you? I mean, *would you*? Wow, Abby, I'd love to take you to the dance. I mean, that is, if you really wanted to go with—"

"Leonard, I'm so sorry," she exclaimed. "I wasn't being very clear. What I meant to say is—"

"Yeah, yeah. Sorry, I misunderstood." Clearly embarrassed, he turned his back to her, focusing his attention back on the computer screen.

"No, that's not what I mean, Leonard." She put a hand on his shoulder and, lowering her voice, leaned over and quickly explained about the blind dates. "So, you see, we're all finding dates for each other. No one knows for sure who they're going with."

"Huh?" He looked up with a bewildered expression.

She grabbed a chair and slid it next to him and sat down. "I mean, you'll have your date all set up. And you and your date would go with our group. But you wouldn't know who the girl was until the night of the dance. Does that make sense?"

"Yeah . . . I guess." He frowned. "So you wouldn't be my date?"

She remembered how Bryn and Devon had said they might leave the guys hanging on this little piece of misinformation. But Abby didn't think that seemed ethical. She shook her head. "No, I wouldn't be your date. Sorry." She smiled. "But I wouldn't have been disappointed if I had been your date. And we'll all be going together, so I might get to dance with you . . . that is, if you were interested in dancing with me."

"Yeah, sure . . . I mean, if I decide to do this." He peered curiously at her. "Do you think it's a good idea?"

Now she felt uncertain. He was such a nice guy. And to put him with Devon? Maybe that was just plain mean. What had she been thinking? She was getting ready to pull the plug and apologize all over again, but then his face brightened.

"I mean, I'd really like to do it," he continued hopefully. "It sounds like it could be fun. And the whole part about dressing up in a costume . . . well, I'm down with that too. So, sure, I'm in. Thanks."

"You'll have to dress up like Romeo," she informed him, hoping that perhaps that might put him off and turn this thing around. Seriously, how many guys would be willing to wear tights? "You know, as in *Romeo and Juliet*. Shakespeare."

"Absolutely." He nodded firmly. "I can do that."

She felt completely torn now. Part of her was thankful that her work here was done and she could get on with her own life, but the other part of her felt guilty, not to mention seriously worried for Leonard's sake. What if Devon ate him alive at the dance? And yet, he'd be in costume, wouldn't he? Maybe Devon wouldn't know who he was. Abby knew that everyone was expected to wear those funny eye masks like an old-fashioned masquerade ball. It was possible that Devon might not even figure out exactly who Leonard was for quite some time. Maybe by the time everyone took off their masks, Devon would be okay with the whole thing. Besides that, with Leonard's dark, curly hair and intense brown eyes, he might make a fairly good-looking Romeo. Really, Abby could've done worse.

"Great," she said as she shook his hand. "You have just won yourself a blind date with the beautiful Juliet." Now she explained how he could probably land himself a costume from the drama department if he got right to it. "Don't let on to anyone else that you're playing Romeo, though," she warned. "You don't want to spoil the surprise. Okay?"

He nodded. "Okay." He gave her a grateful smile. "I wouldn't have agreed to something like this with just anyone. But I feel like I can trust you, Abby. Thanks."

She swallowed hard. "Yes," she said quietly. "You can trust me." But as she went back to her desk, she realized that the pressure was on. She would have to do everything within her power to get the rest of the DG to back her on this, but her mind was made up—no DG members would be allowed to make their blind dates feel bad on the night of the dance. That would be just wrong. And if she had to get this in writing and change their bylaws, she was determined to do so. Because no way was she going to allow Devon to hurt Leonard's feelings. *No way!*

Cassidy was secretly glad to hear that Abby was the next one to secure a blind date. But when Abby started to lobby for a new rule, she was curious. "Why do we need this rule?" she asked as the girls ate lunch together.

"Because I don't want to be part of a mean girls' club," Abby said.

"A mean girls' club?" Devon frowned. "What are you insinuating?"

"I'm saying that when I agreed to be part of the DG, I never thought we'd turn into a bunch of elitist snobs."

"Elitist snobs?" Bryn set her water bottle down with a clunk. "What's that supposed to mean?"

Abby looked Bryn squarely in the eyes. "The way you and Devon were talking the other day, acting like you were too good for someone . . . well, someone like, say, Leonard Mansfield. When I assured you that he's a perfectly nice guy." Abby glanced over at Cassidy and Emma, as if she hoped to garner some support from them. "Anyway, that kind of attitude puts a lot of pressure on some of us, you know?"

"That's true," Emma chimed in. "I don't want to feel like someone in the DG is going to hate me if I don't land her the perfect blind date."

"And I don't like giving others the impression that we're a snobby bunch of mean girls," Abby declared. "That's not what I signed on for with our little club."

"Me too," Cassidy agreed. "But are you sure that we need to make a rule about it? I mean, we already have ten rules and—"

"Fine. Maybe we don't need another rule." Abby turned to Devon and Bryn. "But I'd like to have some kind of assurance that no one in our club will throw a hissy fit if she doesn't wind up with Prince Charming for the masquerade ball."

Bryn rolled her eyes. "Do you really think I'd do that?"

Abby shrugged. "I'd like to think you wouldn't. But to hear you talk . . . well, I'm not so sure."

Bryn laughed sarcastically. "Well, *talk*—as they say—*is cheap*. But if it will calm you down, Abs, I can assure you that I won't throw a hissy fit."

"Really?" Abby looked unconvinced.

"You have my word. If my date turns out to be, well, less than fabulous, I will just grin and bear it. Okay?"

"I guess that's okay." Abby frowned as she pushed a straw into her soda.

Cassidy actually felt a wave of relief—after all, she was the one responsible for Bryn's blind date. Hopefully Bryn meant what she'd said. She glanced at Abby, suddenly wondering if she might be handling Devon's date—and perhaps she'd made a bad choice. Poor Abby—*that* would be stressful. Okay, Cassidy decided, maybe it was time for some DG sisterly support here.

"You know," Cassidy began slowly, "the more I think about it, the more I get what Abby is saying. Maybe we really do need a new rule."

"I thought we were done with that," Bryn said a bit sharply. "I told you guys I'd be civilized." She shook a finger at Abby. "Just don't you go and set me up with a loser, *girlfriend*."

"Who said I'm setting you up with *anyone*?" Abby said in a slightly hurt tone.

"Yeah . . . whatever. But I can read you like a book, *Abbykins*." Bryn laughed as she pushed a long strand of blonde hair over her shoulder. "We've been friends too long. Anyway, I know you'd never do something like that to me."

Abby focused on her lunch without responding and now Cassidy had to bite her tongue to keep from confessing she was the one who'd be setting up Bryn's blind date.

"Let's all make an agreement," Emma said calmly. "I can totally see Abby's point. And I agree that I don't want the DG to become known as a mean girls' clique. Let's all promise to be understanding about our blind dates. Like my mom sometimes tells me when I can't have exactly what I want—*this is what you get, now don't throw a fit*."

Some of them laughed, but Bryn still looked slightly aggravated. "Fine," she said a bit grumpily. "I already said that I agree to this. But I'd like it to go on record that I will be severely disappointed if my date turns out to be a total loser. Especially since I did my very best to get *someone else* their dream date."

"I don't know if I will agree . . ." Devon gave the rest of them a skeptical look. "I'm not sure I like the sound of this.

I don't want to get stuck with a jerk again. I'm barely over the homecoming dance. If I ended up with someone like Jason, I'd—"

"We already agreed to no jerks like Jason," Emma reminded her. "Remember?"

Devon still looked doubtful.

"Maybe we should vote on whether this should become a DG rule," Cassidy suggested. Suddenly she felt the need to nail this thing down. Abby was making a very valid point here. "Everyone in favor of—"

"What if we all just agree to give our word," Bryn suggested. "Then we won't need a new law."

"That works for me," Abby said.

"Okay then . . . all in favor?" Cassidy looked around the table to see Bryn barely lifting a forefinger while Abby and Emma discreetly raised a hand. But Devon had not budged. Her arms were folded across her front.

"Devon?" Abby pointed at her. "Are you saying you don't agree with this?"

"Excuse me, but we've kicked this around so much that I'm not entirely sure what I'm agreeing to." Devon had a slightly sour expression. "Am I swearing that I won't grumble if I draw a dud for the dance?"

Cassidy couldn't help but smile. "We're all agreeing that we will conduct ourselves with good manners, no matter who our dates are." She glanced around the table. "Right?"

"Yeah," Emma said. "This is what you get, now don't throw a fit. Remember?"

"Okay . . ." Devon made an exasperated sigh. And Cassidy asked them to vote again. This time they all agreed—even if Bryn and Devon acted reluctant—but Cassidy recorded it into the minutes and considered it done.

"Okay, now that we've taken care of that stupid business, I want you guys to see this." Bryn pulled her iPad from her purse and started showing them photos of dresses. "These are all from the flapper era," she explained. "I found this great site that sells authentic reproduction dresses. Look at this coral one and all that long fringe and beads. Isn't it awesome?"

"Yeah, that looks like it would be fun to dance in," Abby said.

"And check out this gold one with all the beadwork. I really love it—and since Daisy was the golden girl, it seems perfect."

"Is that the price?" Emma asked in horror. "$1,650?"

"Wowzers." Cassidy shook her head. "You wouldn't actually pay that much for a dress, would you?"

"I wish." Bryn sighed dreamily. "It's so gorgeous. But I already talked to my grandma about sewing me something, and she's really into it. I'll have to buy some shoes. Here, let me show you the ones I found last night." She flipped over to photos of shoes now, explaining which ones would be perfect and why.

"I wonder what kind of shoes Emma Woodhouse would wear," Emma mused as they all watched Bryn sliding through the shoe pictures.

"Slippers," Bryn told her. "Maybe something like a ballet flat." She typed in some words and new photos appeared. "Like these," she held the iPad up for Emma to see better.

"But I can't afford those." Emma pointed to the prices.

"Oh, you can find them for a fraction of that," Bryn told her. "I'll help you."

"How about Cass's ruby slippers?" Abby asked. "Can you find them on there too?"

"I already have that covered," Cassidy told them, explaining how her mom had an old pair of shoes with the right shape. "I'm going to spray paint them red and then I'll glue red glitter all over them."

"Sounds like fun," Abby said.

"Well, at least your shoes will be hot," Bryn teased.

"But that little-girl gingham dress that Dorothy wears . . ." Devon smirked. "Well, good luck with that, Cass."

Cassidy tried not to show that Bryn and Devon's teasing words stung. She knew this was just Devon being Devon, but she didn't appreciate how Bryn seemed to be changing—as if Devon was having too much influence over her. And it was hard not to feel offended by these girls who were supposed to be Cassidy's friends. Maybe instead of making a new rule to prevent meanness toward the blind dates they should've made a rule to prevent meanness toward fellow DG members. Still, Cassidy reminded herself of her recent resolve about Devon. She was not going to get mad at Devon, and she was not going to let Devon get the best of her. As for Bryn, well, maybe Cassidy needed to start thinking of Bryn along the same lines.

As Cassidy walked through the math department, she was still feeling a little out of sorts toward Bryn. But at the same time she could see the irony of her situation. Bryn, who'd been acting like such a spoiled brat and treating Cassidy like she was inferior, had no idea that her date fate was in Cassidy's hands at the moment. For whatever reason, Bryn seemed to assume that Abby was setting her up. But Cassidy had drawn Bryn's name—and she was in complete control of who would be Bryn's blind date.

Cassidy chuckled to herself. Okay then, if Bryn was going

to start acting like an entitled snob . . . well, maybe it was time to test their little agreement. Would Bryn throw a hissy fit if her date turned out to be, say, *Darrell Zuckerman*?

To be fair, Darrell Zuckerman wasn't so bad. Cassidy had known him for years. In fact, unless her memory was failing her, Bryn was already well acquainted with Darrell. Cassidy was pretty sure he was Bryn's lab partner. And Bryn had even recommended Darrell for someone else's date for homecoming. Sure, maybe she was teasing at the time. Or else it might've been a Freudian way for Bryn to suggest that she wanted a date with Zuckerman herself.

Cassidy had Darrell in her next class. And just like that, she decided—*why not?* After all, everyone knew that Darrell Zuckerman was brilliant—he supposedly had a genius IQ—so Bryn couldn't complain about that. Okay, it was no secret that besides being an academic nerd, Darrell was also a rather outspoken atheist. A bit of an oddity at a Christian school. But rumor had it that he was only enrolled at Northwood because his devout parents had hoped that the experience would transform him. And perhaps a date with the beautiful Bryn Jacobs might hasten that transformation. Or not. Cassidy giggled to herself as she spotted Darrell leaning against a column outside of the civics classroom.

Okay, Cassidy knew that, despite being in a churchgoing family, Bryn did not take her faith seriously. Perhaps that was a good thing—what would she care if her date didn't believe in God? If nothing else, it might give Bryn something to think about. Maybe she would take a better look at her own spiritual state of affairs. Or maybe she would start learning how to treat her friends better.

"Hey, Darrell," Cassidy said casually as she went over to

him. His shaggy brown hair was hanging over one eye, but his face lit up with a grin.

"Hey, Cass." He stood a little straighter. "What's up?"

"Not much." She decided to get right to the point. "So are you going to the masquerade ball?"

He laughed. "Oh, yeah, sure. I plan to dress up like Satan and crash the festive little soiree. How about you?"

"Satan?" She frowned. "We're supposed to go as literary characters."

"What about that big book you all believe in? Wasn't Satan in the Bible? And what about *Paradise Lost*? He was in there."

Cassidy forced a smile. "Well, that's interesting. So I guess you wouldn't be into going to the dance with a girl."

"A girl?" His dark brows arched. "What *kind* of girl?"

"One of my friends," she said enticingly.

"Your friends?" He sounded suspicious. "Kind of like last time, when you chicks tried to set me up with Devon?"

Cassidy slowly shook her head. "Yeah, that was a big mistake, Darrell. And I've already told you I'm sorry about how that went down." She made a sincere smile. "I like to think that we're friends."

He studied her closely. "And a friend doesn't mess with a friend, right?"

Suddenly she questioned herself. What on earth was she doing? Maybe it was time to back out. But what could she say?

"Well, I guess I might be open to taking one of your friends to the ball," he said slowly. "As long as this isn't some kind of trick." He scowled at her. "You wouldn't do that to me, would you? Set me up with Devon again?"

"No way."

"Who is it then?" Darrell was still frowning, but she could hear the distinct tone of interest in his tone.

"I can't tell you who." She bit her lip, wondering how she could get out of this gracefully. "I get why that might be a problem for you, Darrell. I would totally understand if you're not interested." She nervously explained the whole blind date idea and how they would all go together. The whole time he listened with what seemed to be growing and genuine interest. "So you won't find out who your date is until the big night."

"Really?" He nodded with approval. "Very cool."

"Yeah?" She tried not to look too shocked . . . or worried.

"So am I supposed to dress in costume too?"

"That's right. You would actually come as Jay Gatsby."

"From *The Great Gatsby*?" He rubbed his chin thoughtfully. "A rather tragic character. Hmm . . . I'm liking this more and more."

The warning bell was ringing, which meant they had one minute. "So are you in?" she asked nervously, almost hoping he'd change his mind.

"You really won't tell me who the girl is? Which of your friends?"

"Only that it's not Devon." She started for the door and paused. "I'll tell you this much, Darrell. You know her. And she's pretty. Is that enough?"

He grinned. "Enough for me." Grasping her by the arm, he stopped her from going inside the classroom. "You're not jerking my chain, are you, Cassidy? Because if you are . . . well, trust me, I can get even. You don't want that. Not after the last time with Devon. I'm a tolerant guy, but there's a limit to my patience. This is a real date, isn't it?"

"It's a real date," she told him. "I promise."

He looked intently into her eyes. "Okay, I believe you. But be warned, if this is a scam or you're punking me, you *will* be sorry."

She held her hand up like an oath. "Honest, Darrell. This is for real." She glanced over her shoulder to see if anyone was watching this little spectacle. "I'll give you all the rest of the details later. But for now you just figure out how Jay Gatsby would dress. Okay?"

With a creased brow, as if he was giving this careful thought, he released her arm. "Okay." A smile crept onto his lips. "This could be fun."

As Cassidy took her seat in civics she felt a mixture of anxiety, relief, fear, and shock. She was glad that was over with, but at the same time she wondered if she'd gone too far by asking Darrell. Not only because of Bryn's possible reaction. But she hadn't expected Darrell to act quite like that. Then again, why wouldn't he, after what had happened with Devon? Darrell Zuckerman was hard to read about some things, but she got his message plain and clear. If the blind date turned out badly for him, he would seek revenge—*on her.*

She also knew that just because the DG had verbally agreed not to overreact in regard to their blind dates, it did not guarantee that Bryn wouldn't show some displeasure about being matched up with Darrell Zuckerman. Cassidy had seen Bryn turn her nose up before, and she could imagine her acting snooty and superior to Darrell.

Cassidy studied Darrell's back. He might not be tall, but he was solid. He had a square, rocklike appearance from behind. And she couldn't forget the steely look of resolve in those gray-blue eyes. What if Bryn really hurt his feelings? What might he do to get even with Cassidy? Was it too late to undo this? Was there any way to get out of the situation gracefully? She bit the end of her pencil, trying to think of some convenient escape. Maybe she could come down with a mysterious case of the flu right before the dance.

Or maybe she could simply offer to trade blind dates with Bryn. She had no idea who her date would end up being or who was setting her up. At the moment, she didn't even care. How could Bryn complain if Cassidy was willing to sacrifice herself like that for Bryn's sake? Somehow Cassidy had to come up with a plan to erase the mess she'd just created.

As she opened her notebook, she made up her mind that the best plan would be to go out with Darrell herself. It might not be much fun, but it would be preferable to turning a slightly diabolical genius into a sworn enemy. Because she wasn't quite sure how he would do it, but she felt certain that Darrell Zuckerman could easily derail her life.

Earlier in the week, Devon hadn't felt overly concerned about lining up a blind date for Cassidy. After all, it wasn't like she had to tell the guy who he'd be taking—especially since everyone knew that Cass wasn't exactly hot. But by Thursday morning, after Devon discovered that Lane Granger was going to be out of town the weekend of the dance and that Isaac McKinley already had a date—not to mention that Bryn, Abby, and even Cassidy had all secured blind dates—Devon was starting to feel desperate. She knew that unless she wanted to be the last girl to lock up a guy, it was time to scramble.

She'd briefly considered asking Harris Martin—mostly because he was such a hottie and any excuse to talk to him seemed like a good excuse. Except that, at the same time, she was actually hoping that someone in the DG might be setting her up with Harris. She didn't want to do anything to mess that up. She'd already hinted to her friends that he'd be her first choice—more than once. For some reason she thought maybe Emma was arranging her blind date, and she'd spied Emma talking to Harris just yesterday. Naturally, Devon had dropped even more hints to Emma this morning. However, Emma had been pretty tight-lipped.

"I will tell you this much," Emma had confided. "The guy I've been talking with has promised to give me his answer today."

Naturally, that made Devon feel even more driven to get her assignment completed. She hated the idea of coming in last place in this. She knew it wasn't a contest—not really—but Devon was so competitive that she had a tendency to turn lots of things into contests.

Anyway, there was still Kent Renner, Devon reminded herself as she walked toward the gym that afternoon. Oh, she knew that Abby liked Kent and that she was probably secretly hoping to be set up with him, but like they'd all agreed, this blind date thing was supposed to be a surprise. Wouldn't Cassidy—and Abby—be surprised if Devon talked him into being Cass's blind date?

And since Kent was in Devon's weight-training class, she decided this was her perfect opportunity. However, when she mentioned the dance to Kent, it sounded as if he was already planning to go. "Who are you taking?" she boldly asked.

"None of your business," he retorted as he adjusted the weight amount on the bench press, then turned his back to her.

"Whatever." She shrugged and walked away, pretending like she didn't care. However, she still was curious. Who was he taking? And how would Abby react when she found out about it? Well, that wasn't Devon's problem. As she got herself a spot in the circuit-training group, she tried to think of another guy that she could ask for Cassidy. Before the day was done, she was determined to settle this.

"So . . . you're looking for someone to go to the masquerade ball?" a guy she hadn't met asked. She could tell he was trying to act casual, but he looked nervous and his Adam's apple bobbed up and down as he swallowed.

With her hands on her hips, she studied him. He was definitely nerdish looking with his bad haircut, pale skin, long nose, and less-than-stylish workout clothes. He was probably taking weight training in the hopes of building some muscles—which would be a major improvement. "I'm sorry," she said, feigning ignorance. "Were you talking to me?"

"Yeah." He smiled, revealing slightly crooked teeth as he continued to pump the dumbbells toward his scrawny chest. "I'm Russell Winslow. And I know your name is Devon. Anyway, I just started at Northwood last week. My dad got transferred here. So I don't really know anyone."

"Oh, yeah, you didn't seem familiar." She was trying not to sound too friendly. Why encourage him?

"I know . . . and it's not real easy making new friends."

She softened a little. "I get that. I just started here this fall."

"So we're both new. That's cool." He nodded as he switched positions with the dumbbells. "But I'd think that, well, someone like you . . . I mean, you shouldn't have a hard time getting a date to the dance."

"Thanks." As she bent down to pick up the pair of five-pound dumbbells, she suddenly realized the opportunity knocking on her door. Sure, maybe Devon would never dream of going out with a geeky guy like this herself—but why not get him for Cassidy? Especially since Cassidy had been so supportive of Abby's crazy idea to make a no-complaint rule. Devon suppressed the urge to laugh at this idea. It would be seriously entertaining to see how Cass would react to a guy like Russell. And so, as Devon pumped the weights, she explained the blind date plan, making it clear to Russell that he would not be Devon's date.

"I can assure you that the girl you'd go with is super nice. In fact, I'm certain you're gonna like her," she huffed.

"Really?" He set down his dumbbells, wiping sweat from his brow with the back of his hand.

"She's a nice person," Devon assured him breathlessly. "Very academic. On Honor Society."

"That sounds good." But he still looked slightly uncertain as he picked up the exercise bands, fumbling to loop them around his shoes.

"And she's pretty too." Okay, that might be stretching it. Oh sure, Cass was good-looking in a girl-next-door sort of way. And she was rather attractive when she fixed herself up. But hot she was not. At least not in Devon's opinion.

"Great," he told her. "It sounded a little strange at first. But I really think I'd like to do this."

As she picked up a set of bands, she explained the group date plan and how the guys would coordinate their costumes with the girls. "You down with that?" she asked as she stretched against the bands' resistance.

"So what am I supposed to dress like?"

She shrugged. "I don't know. Something from *The Wizard of Oz*. My friend plans to go as Dorothy."

"Cool. I really like *Oz*."

"So does she." Devon felt amused. Maybe this was a match made in heaven.

"I think I'll go as the scarecrow." Russell's smile grew wider. "Thanks, Devon. This is going to be fun."

She promised to keep him informed of their plans as the dance date got nearer. "And you need to remember that this is all top secret," she said finally. "None of the girls know who they're going with until the big night."

"That works for me."

As Devon continued her workout, she felt quite pleased with herself. Oh, she knew that Cassidy might not be so pleased when she discovered who was taking her to the dance, but that wouldn't happen until the night of the dance. And then Devon would simply remind her of what Emma had said. "This is what you get, now don't throw a fit!"

Devon threw her head back and laughed as she walked back to the locker room. This was going to be good!

• ● ● ● •

"I got my blind date all set," Emma announced as the five of them gathered in the locker bay after school. "Well, not *my* date . . ." She giggled. "But a date for some lucky girl."

"Lucky girl?" Devon said with interest. Hopefully Emma meant her and hopefully Emma meant Harris. "Well, Little Miss Emma wasn't the only one to nail down a blind date today," she told them.

"So everyone got a blind date lined up?" Bryn said happily. "We're all set to go?"

"Except for our costumes," Cassidy said.

"Some of us already have our costumes," Devon bragged.

"And some of us don't," Cassidy told her. "I looked through the drama department's collection and couldn't find anything that would.work for Dorothy."

"But I found this long Empire waist gown that's perfect for the eighteenth century," Emma said. "It has blue-and-white stripes and is really similar to one of the costumes that Gwyneth Paltrow wore in the movie. I'm just going to add some ribbons. And then I want to figure out how to make a bonnet."

"My outfit's coming together too," Abby told them.

"Are you still planning to wear the Katniss hunter clothes?" Bryn asked with a wrinkled nose.

"Yeah. My mom's loaning me this leather jacket that's perfect, and I've got these boots that—"

"Can't we talk you into wearing one of the glamorous costumes?" Bryn begged. "The thing I liked best about that film was when Katniss and Peeta got all dressed up for the ceremonies. She looked so beautiful. And I know my grandma would help us make one. Don't you want to look elegant and feminine and alluring?"

Abby firmly shook her head. "I'm doing this *my* way, Bryn." Now she smiled. "But thanks for the offer."

"I wish I had a grandmother that knew how to sew," Cassidy said glumly.

"My grandma can probably help you," Bryn offered.

"Really?"

"Sure, why not? I'll bet your Dorothy costume would be easy to make."

"Will you ask her?"

Bryn pulled out her phone. "Yeah."

Soon she was talking to her grandma about the Dorothy costume. "Great, Gram, I'll let her know." She hung up her phone and grinned at Cassidy. "She says to come on over to her house with me on Saturday. She actually adores

The Wizard of Oz and thinks it's great that you want to be Dorothy." Bryn shook her head like this was unbelievable. "And she said she might even have some gingham fabric that would work."

"Seriously?" Cassidy looked stunned.

"Do you think your grandma can help me with the bonnet?" Emma asked.

"I'm sure she could." Bryn nodded. "She's really creative with sewing. She doesn't even use patterns a lot of the time. She just knows how to do it."

"I wonder if she could help me make my arrow quiver look like the one in the movie," Abby said tentatively. "I think that might require some sewing."

Bryn grinned. "I have an idea. Let's all storm Gram's house on Saturday. She'd love it. We can all help each other with our costumes. It'll be fun."

Devon was feeling slightly left out. Her Juliet costume—which had been made by Bryn's grandmother—was perfect. It didn't need anything done to it. Besides that, it had already been a bone of contention as far as Bryn was concerned—she'd been so jealous when she'd heard that Devon had already snagged it from the drama department. No need to bring it up again.

But as the other girls discussed what time and what they might need to bring on Saturday morning, Devon was trying to think of a way to involve herself—without actually inviting herself. "I know," she said suddenly. "We should all have a dress rehearsal with our costumes. You know, to make sure everyone looks good. Maybe on Saturday?"

Bryn gave her a slightly blank look. "Well, yeah . . . but I'm not sure that mine will be done by then. There's a lot of beadwork, you know. Gram said it probably wouldn't be finished until right before the dance."

"Oh." Devon shrugged. "Well, it's no big deal. I'm sure we'll all look fine."

Cassidy looked at Devon now. "I guess your costume doesn't need anything, huh?"

"Not really."

"Maybe you should come on Saturday to help us," Cassidy suggested. "With that much sewing to do, I'm sure any extra hands would be welcome."

"That's true," Bryn told her. "The beadwork on my dress alone is really time consuming. You could help me with that."

"Okay." Devon tried not to show how relieved she was to be included in this. The truth was, she had not been getting along with her mother all week—ever since Mom had returned from her unexpected trip to Vegas. The standoff had begun with the silent treatment from Devon. She thought her plan to punish Mom by not talking would teach her a lesson.

That worked the first day, but then Mom had turned the tables on Devon by ignoring her completely. Not only that, but the last couple of days she had gone out with Rodney after work, not coming home until well after midnight last night. Devon wondered how Mom would feel if Devon started to act like that. And if Devon's friends weren't such goody-two-shoes, maybe she would. As it was, Devon's most interesting social engagement this weekend appeared to be attending an all-female sewing circle. This was so wrong. Yet to be perfectly honest, Devon had felt grateful to be included.

Bryn felt proud—perhaps even slightly smug—that she'd managed to snag Emma's main crush for her blind date. Despite Emma's pretense that she and Isaac McKinley were "just friends," Bryn knew that Emma really, really liked the boy. And, to be fair, Isaac was a sweet guy. Bryn knew that he'd make a perfect Mr. Knightley. For that reason, she took him aside right before lunch on Friday—to give him some advice in regard to his costume.

"I'll send you some photos I found online," she was explaining to him. "To give you ideas for how to put together a Mr. Knightley costume."

"You mean I can't wear jeans and a T-shirt?" he teased.

"You're not playing James Dean, silly," she pointed out. "Anyway, you see what you can come up with in the drama department costumes. Try to find something that looks like the photos I'll send you. And, if you need to, just take some photos and send them back to me, and I'll see what I can do to help make it look more authentic."

He beamed at her. "Thanks, Bryn. It's nice of you to help me like this. And thanks for setting me up with, uh, with *Emma*."

Bryn blinked in surprise. "You *know*?"

He laughed. "Now I do."

"What do you mean? What's going on?"

"Hearing that my date was playing the character Emma, well, I just guessed it was Emma Parks."

"Oh." Bryn frowned. "It was supposed to be a surprise—for everyone. Now it's ruined."

"It's not ruined," he assured her. "I'd been thinking of asking Emma myself, but, well, you know . . . that speech Mr. Worthington gave . . . I'm still trying to wrap my head around this whole dating thing."

"You and all the rest of the guys in this school." Bryn wasn't sure exactly what Mr. Worthington had told the boys at the start of school. Well, besides that they should avoid dating and girls in general—which was perfectly ridiculous.

"So I'm really not supposed to say anything to Emma?"

"That's what makes it a blind date—at least for Emma."

"I heard that some girls are following your example to do the blind date thing too," he said.

"Where'd you hear that?" Bryn glanced around the noisy cafeteria. Had the DG started a trend?

"From some of the other guys. It's kind of a cool idea really. I mean, it takes some pressure off of us."

"Well, remember it's all top secret until the night of the dance. No one, especially Emma, is supposed to know."

He nodded. "Got that."

As they parted ways, Bryn recovered from her guilt at blowing Emma's cover. In fact, as she walked to class, she felt rather pleased with herself for making such a good match. In a week, Emma would be most grateful, and Bryn would enjoy basking in that glory. Plus, if there was any truth to karma, then Bryn's blind date for the dance should end up being someone really special. Maybe Marcus Zimmerman—she'd heard he was a good dancer, and she'd been dropping hints about him. But she would also settle for Kent Renner, who actually looked a bit like the Great Gatsby, or even Lane Granger, although she would be a little disappointed. Bryn felt fairly certain that Abby was setting her up—and she felt even more certain that Abby had secured Marcus for her. And, really, why wouldn't she?

"What's up with you and Isaac?" Devon asked Bryn when she sat down at the lunch table with the others.

"Huh?" Bryn gave her an innocent look.

"We all saw you just now," Devon told Bryn. She tipped her head toward Emma. "And I'm not naming names, but someone at this table was watching you like a hawk."

"I was not," Emma declared.

"Yes you were," Devon shot back.

"What difference does it make?" Cassidy asked. "We were all watching."

"Am I not allowed to have a friendly little conversation with a boy without attracting all this undo attention?" Bryn asked primly. She opened her bag lunch from home and pulled out a Greek yogurt and a bag of veggie sticks.

"Of course you are," Emma growled at her.

"Ooh, you are mad," Bryn said back. "Is this how you treat your friends?"

Emma glared at her. "What about how you treat your friends?" she demanded. "And what about the DG rules?"

"What rules?" Bryn asked nonchalantly.

"Never mind," Emma grumbled.

But Bryn was feeling indignant now. All she'd been doing was trying to help Emma—and this was the thanks she got? "You mean the rule about *not stealing boyfriends*? As far as I can see none of the DG members have a boyfriend." She glanced around the table. "Am I wrong about that?" No one responded.

"But everyone knows that Emma likes Isaac," Cassidy said quietly.

"I do not!" Emma declared.

"Ooh, methinks you protest too much," Bryn said.

"Why are you talking like that?" Emma demanded. "You sound like you've been trapped in a Jane Austen novel too long."

"Hey, I thought you liked Jane Austen," Bryn teased.

"I *used* to." Emma stood and picked up her tray. "Excuse me!"

"Wow." Bryn slowly shook her head. "Sounds like someone's having a bad PMS day."

"Oh, Bryn." Cassidy gave her a disgusted look. "Why'd you have to tease her like that?"

"She attacked me first," Bryn said defensively. "All I was doing was talking to Isaac and—"

"It looked more like you were flirting," Cassidy clarified. "And Emma got really hurt before . . . when she, uh, thought someone else was flirting with Isaac."

"Who?" Abby asked.

"It doesn't matter." Cassidy tossed a slightly accusing look Devon's way.

"*Moi?*" Devon asked innocently.

"If the shoe fits." Cassidy was gathering up her lunch things now.

"Emma said I was flirting with Isaac?" Devon gave a fake-looking shocked expression. "Since when?"

"I don't know exactly." Cassidy let out a frustrated sigh as she stood with her tray. "All I know is that Emma might pretend she's not into Isaac, but she really is." She looked directly at Bryn now. "And if you care about Emma and consider yourself her friend, you should respect that. You shouldn't try to hurt her."

"Why's she so thin-skinned?" Bryn asked. "And why does she pretend not to like Isaac when she obviously does? And why does she get all hurt when one of us talks to him?"

Cassidy pressed her lips together. "You really want to know the answer to all that?"

"Yes," Bryn declared. "As a matter of fact I do."

"Okay . . . I think it's because her dad left her." Cassidy made an uneasy glance at Devon. "And I realize Emma's not the only one whose parents have split. But I know that Emma is very sensitive. I think you all know that. And I think she's worried that if she gets too involved with Isaac—even though she really likes him—well, she's afraid he will hurt her too. Just like her dad."

"Since when did you turn junior psychologist?" Devon asked.

"I think that makes sense," Abby said.

"So maybe before you start teasing her, you should consider that," Cassidy said to Bryn. And then she left.

"Wow." Bryn let out a long sigh. "Sure didn't see that coming."

• • ● • •

Bryn wasn't sure what to expect on Saturday morning. After experiencing Emma's wrath like that—which was, by the way, totally unjust—and after getting lectured by Cassidy in front of the group, Bryn didn't know if her friends would even show up at Gram's for sewing assistance today. And she wasn't sure that she cared.If these girls were going to start acting all crazy and overly sensitive and hormonal, well, maybe it was best to part ways. The club had been fun while it lasted, but maybe it was time to call it a day. And, really, did Bryn even need the DG? She suspected that without their blind date plan, she would've gotten a date to the dance anyway. And probably a lot sooner—and with a lot less trouble too.

However, as she got into the car, she knew that she would miss the DG if it disintegrated. Hopefully the girls had moved on by now. It was silly to let an innocent conversation with a guy split them up like that. Especially just one week before this dance—which could turn out to be pretty cool. Bryn had loved dressing up in costumes ever since she was old enough to slide her feet into her mom's heels and drape herself in her scarves and jewelry. And she was determined not to let a little disagreement spoil their fun now. Besides that, Gram was looking forward to having the other girls there today. She had even suggested having pizza delivered for lunch.

Bryn wondered if she should pull over and call Emma right now. But to do what? Apologize? And for what? *Bryn had done nothing wrong!* If anyone owed somebody an apology, it was Emma. But since Emma obviously didn't realize her mistake—not yet anyway—well, maybe Bryn would have to take this one on the chin so to speak. A week from now, when Emma found out that Bryn had set her up with Isaac and even helped Isaac with his costume, all would be forgiven.

As she pulled up to Abby's house, Bryn hoped that her supposed best friend was feeling more congenial today. Abby had given Bryn a second lecture on the way home from school yesterday. For some reason Abby had gotten it into her head that Bryn had been acting like a snob lately. All because of that business with Isaac? It was ridiculous, of course. And Bryn had tried to straighten Abby out—without going into the top-secret blind date details—but Abby hadn't seemed to want to listen.

When Abby got into the car, she didn't seem like her usual cheerful self. Bryn tried to make small talk, but Abby was acting pretty quiet as Bryn drove them across town to her grandmother's house.

"Are you still mad at me?" Bryn asked as she stopped for a traffic light.

"Mad at you?" Abby said absently. "Why?"

"Because I hurt Emma's feelings yesterday. Because you think I'm a snob."

"Oh, that . . . Well, like I said, I didn't particularly like it," Abby admitted. "But, no, I'm not still mad at you."

"Is something wrong then?"

"I don't know . . ."

"There *is* something wrong," Bryn declared. "Is it me?"

"I already said that it's not."

"What is it then?" Bryn demanded.

Abby let out a loud sigh. "I can't tell you."

"What do you mean *you can't tell me*?" Bryn glanced at Abby as the light turned green. "I thought we were best friends. How is it possible you can keep something from me?"

"If you must know, it has to do with the blind date biz. But it's supposed to be secret, remember?"

"Oh . . ." Bryn slowly nodded, taking this in. "So you really did set me up then? And you're worried because you set me up with someone you think I might not be so happy with?"

"Good grief, Bryn. Everything is not always all about you,"

Abby said. "Do you know how narcissistic you can sound sometimes?"

"Narcissistic?" Bryn pushed her lower lip out. "That's a little harsh."

"Sorry. You're right. But, seriously, Bryn, *it's not always about you.*"

"So, you're telling me that you didn't arrange my blind date? Because I'm pretty sure I know that you did. And if you tell me the truth, I promise not to breathe a word of it to anyone. It will be our secret."

"Well, I hate to disappoint you, but you are wrong. I set up—uh—someone else." Abby put her hand over her mouth. "Crud. I didn't even mean to say that much."

"No big deal. It's not like you told me who you did set up." Bryn lowered her voice as if someone else was listening even though it was just the two of them in the car. "But you could tell me, Abby. I would keep it a secret. You can trust me."

Abby firmly shook her head.

"Okay then . . . maybe you can tell me *why* you're freaking over whatever it is you're freaking over."

"You promise you won't breathe a word of this to anyone?"

"You know I won't," Bryn assured her. "Think of all the other secrets I've kept for you over the years."

"Well . . . I'm kinda worried about the blind date I got for—uh—the DG member whose name I can't mention."

"Uh-huh?"

"I'm sure she's going to be pretty upset about the guy. I mean, I know she's going to be really ticked at me. And I'll admit that it was really impulsive on my part."

"Interesting. So you set someone up with a real loser, huh?" Bryn asked. "Someone who thankfully is not me."

"I know it was a huge mistake. But I have no idea how to undo it."

"Just tell the loser dude that you changed your mind. Or made a mistake. Or whatever. And then ask someone else more appropriate."

"But it will hurt the guy's feelings. He was so happy about going to the dance. And he's already gotten his costume together. I can't do that to him, Bryn."

"Then I suppose you have to suffer the consequences, huh?"

"I suppose so."

Bryn was about to guess who was getting stuck with the blind-date-loser-dude, but she was already at her grandma's house. "Hey, look, there's Cassidy's car. It looks like Emma and Devon are with her too."

"Yeah, why wouldn't they be?"

"Because they were so mad at me yesterday?"

"Oh, well . . . maybe the members are taking the second rule seriously."

"What's the second rule?"

"To be loyal to fellow DG members." Abby sighed as she opened the door. "I read over the rules last night."

"So do you think you were being loyal when you set someone up with a loser?" Bryn asked quietly as they got out of the car.

"Shhh!" Abby warned. "Don't remind me."

As Bryn went over to greet her friends, she reassured herself that all was well. The DG was all here, and they had obviously decided to let bygones be bygones.

I gotta take this." Emma held up her phone as the five of them were walking up to Bryn's grandmother's two-story brick house. "I'll be done in a minute." She waited for the others to go inside.

"Hey, Kent," she said into her phone. "What's up?"

"You promised to send me some costume ideas," he told her. "Remember?"

"Oh, yeah. I put some photos on my phone. I can send them right now if you want. Or else you could rent the movie."

"That's a chick flick," he said in a disdainful tone.

"A chick flick? Are you kidding? *The Hunger Games* is about a bunch of people killing each other. It's all about this horrible fight where only one person is supposed to survive. It is absolutely not a chick flick, Kent."

"Seriously?"

"Absolutely. Watch the movie, Kent. You're going to like it." Now, without giving away Abby's name, Emma described the outfit Abby planned to wear. "She'll even be carrying a bow with her. And I don't mean a bow in her hair. A bow-and-arrow kind of bow. Anyway, as Peeta, you should wear something that goes with that kind of outfit."

"Okay. I guess that works for me. I didn't like the idea of having to rent a tux or something like that."

"And I can't remember if I told you, but there will be ten of us sharing the limo—"

"Kind of like for homecoming?"

"Yeah. And we'll split the cost ten ways."

"Sounds good."

She went over a few more details, then promised to send the photos. "But you make sure you rent that movie—"

"I don't have to rent it, my little sister owns it."

"Well, then borrow her DVD—and do your homework." She chuckled. "Now here come the photos." She sent him the photos and then hurried into the house where Bryn's grandfather greeted her, then directed her toward some stairs. She went down to find everyone gathered in a finished basement, a well-lit space that Bryn's grandmother used as her sewing and craft room.

"And this is Emma," Bryn told a tall woman with short platinum hair. "Emma, this is my grandmother, Mrs. Jacobs."

"Pleased to meet you," Emma said as she gazed at the floor-to-ceiling shelves, all neatly filled with fabrics and craft supplies and plastic crates and all sorts of interesting-looking stuff. "Wow, it looks like you have everything down here."

"My husband would agree with you on that," Mrs. Jacobs said.

As Mrs. Jacobs showed the girls around the amazing room, pointing out the various craft areas and cutting tables along with three different sewing machines, Emma felt a small wave of jealousy. How cool would it be to have a grandma like this? Especially since Emma had always been into art and creating things. Ironically, Emma's own grandmother didn't have a creative bone in her body. At least none that Emma knew of. Grandma's favorite activity was to go to the bingo parlor or watch TV game shows. But thinking of her grandma like that made Emma feel guilty—especially considering how Grandma was feeling so lonely and still grieving over Grandpa's recent death. For that matter, so was Emma. Just one more thing that seemed unfair.

"You're lucky that your grandma has all this stuff," Emma told Bryn as Mrs. Jacobs showed Cassidy some blue-and-white gingham fabric that she thought would be perfect for the Dorothy dress.

"I guess so." Bryn shrugged. "Gram is a pretty crafty old gal."

"You could make almost anything down here."

"Yeah, and I'm pretty sure Gram has made almost everything you can imagine." Now Bryn held up a gold-colored dress that had strings of glittering beads in the process of being attached. "This is my Daisy dress." She pointed out where the rest of the beadwork would go. "It's going to be really cool."

"It's absolutely gorgeous." Once again Emma could feel herself stifling the waves of jealousy that were rising up within her. Was Bryn trying to make her feel bad or did she just have no clue? Well, even if it hurt, Emma was determined to be courteous to Bryn today. After all, Bryn was kind of like the hostess here. Emma was her guest. Besides that, Emma was feeling a little embarrassed over her display of emotion yesterday. She still wasn't sure what had gotten into her. Besides jealousy, that is. Yet here she was feeling green with envy all over again. Only this time she wasn't jealous over a boy, she was jealous over a grandma. Really, it was lame. And sad. And pathetic. *Get over yourself*, she silently chided herself. *You're here to have fun.*

• • ● • •

It soon became clear that despite how clever and creative she was, Mrs. Jacobs had her hands full with five girls in her basement. Finally, after she had shown Emma how she might make an old-fashioned bonnet and even given her some materials, Emma decided to attempt this project on her own.

"Don't you need a ride?" Cassidy asked with pins sticking out of her mouth.

"That's okay," Emma explained. "I called my grandma and she's picking me up in a few minutes."

Cassidy nodded, focusing on the blue-and-white gingham pieces that she was getting ready to sew together. "Okay."

Emma thanked Bryn and her grandmother, then went upstairs and outside to wait for Grandma.

"What are you doing out here?" Bryn's grandfather looked surprised to see her as he came around the corner from the garage with a partially coiled garden hose in his hands.

Emma made an uneasy smile. "I'm waiting for my grandma to pick me up."

"Everything okay?" he asked with a concerned expression.

"Yes." She nodded. "It was just a little crowded down there. And I was, uh, thinking about my own grandma. I thought maybe she'd like to help me with this." She held up the plastic bag containing the bonnet materials. "You see, she's been kind of lonely since my grandpa died."

He nodded with compassion. "I'm sorry for your loss."

Now she felt embarrassed for saying so much. "Yeah . . . thanks."

"That's nice that you want to spend time with your grandmother. I'm sure she'll appreciate the company."

Emma spied Grandma's old Buick coming down the street. "There she is now." She gave him a big smile. "Thanks for letting us invade your home."

He chuckled as he continued coiling the hose. "Anytime."

Emma hurried down to her grandma's car, eagerly hopping inside where it was warm and smelled like french fries.

"I was at McDonald's when you called." Grandma pointed to the bag next to her. "Help yourself."

Emma giggled as she reached for what Grandma usually called her worst vice. "Thanks."

"So what do you need help with?" Grandma asked as she turned down her street.

Emma explained how she was dressing up as Jane Austen's Emma and how she wanted to make a bonnet to go with her costume. "Did you ever read the book?" she asked.

Grandma shook her head. "You know I'm not much of a reader, Emma."

Emma reached into her bag where she'd tucked the DVD that Cassidy had loaned her. "I have the movie," she said. "We could watch it if you want. I wanted to get a better look at the bonnets Emma wears."

"That's a great idea," Grandma agreed. "I'd like that."

As they went into the house, Emma tried not to look at the recliner that her grandpa used to sit in to watch football games. Instead, she described the dress she was going to wear in detail. "And the hat is supposed to have this really wide brim," she explained, "with ribbons coming down on both sides." She held up the DVD. "But you'll see it when we watch the movie."

Together they watched the movie while Emma worked on the hat, following the directions that Mrs. Jacobs had given her. "I think this looks pretty good," she told her grandmother when the movie finally ended. Then, placing it on her head, Emma stood up and modeled it around the family room.

"That's perfect," Grandma told her. "It's almost exactly like the one in the movie. You're such a clever girl, Emma. Such an artist."

Emma went over to the wall mirror and nodded in satisfaction. "It really does look like the one in the movie." Now she frowned. "But my hair isn't long enough to braid it like Gwyneth Paltrow did."

"I have an idea." Grandma stood up. "Come with me."

Emma followed Grandma to the master bedroom where Grandma started digging through her closet. "My hair used to be the same color as yours," Grandma said as she pulled down some boxes from a high shelf. "And back when I was in my twenties, I had this fall."

"A fall? What's a fall?"

Grandma laughed. "It's a hairpiece that you attached to the top of your head to make it look like you had long hair." She opened a pink box, and digging through some old scarves and things, she eventually produced what looked like a blondish ponytail. "Here it is." She swung it around. "My fall."

Emma giggled at the strange-looking hair. "You really wore that?"

"Just for one summer. It was during the late sixties and all the girls had long hair and I thought I wanted to look like them. You put it on the top of your head, then wrapped a scarf or hair band around to conceal where it connected." She held it up to her head, then looked into the mirror inside her closet and broke into laughter. "Oh, my goodness. It looks about as bad now as it did back then."

Emma couldn't help but laugh too. Grandma looked ridiculous with that scraggly blonde hair hanging down over her short gray hair.

"But I thought that we might be able to braid it," Grandma said as she led Emma out into the bedroom. She went over to her dressing table and picked up a brush to smooth out the hair before separating it into three strands. "Here, you hold this end while I braid it."

Emma watched as Grandma worked the hair into a fairly smooth-looking braid. "Now stand still," Grandma told Emma, positioning her in front of the big mirror. Using bobby pins and hair gel, she smoothed most of Emma's hair back, leaving a few feathered bangs to frame her face. Then she wrapped the thick braid around her head like a crown and secured it in place. "How's that?"

"Oh, Grandma!" Emma exclaimed. "It looks just like the movie."

"Let's try it with your bonnet," Grandma said with enthusiasm.

Soon Emma had on the bonnet, and she couldn't have been happier. "It's perfect, Grandma."

Grandma had her camera out now. "Let's get a photo of it. I want to send this to Aunt Lucy."

Emma posed for her. "I wish I had the dress here so we could see how all of it looks together."

"I wish you did too." Grandma took another shot.

"Hey, why don't you come over to our house on Friday? That's the night of the dance," Emma suggested. "That way you can see how I look with everything all together."

Grandma's eyes lit up. "That would be wonderful, dear. I'd love that."

"Great," Emma told her. "It's a date."

"Speaking of dates." Grandma looked at the clock. "I promised to pick up Marsha for bingo tonight. Can I give you a lift home?"

As Emma gathered up her things, she thanked Grandma for helping her.

"Oh, I didn't really do anything," Grandma said as they went out to the car. "You know I'm not very creative, sweetie. You made the bonnet all by yourself."

"But you were encouraging to me," Emma told her. "And you watched the movie with me, and you're the one who thought of using the fall for my braid. That was creative and it's going to make my costume way better."

"I guess we make a good team," Grandma said as she started the car. "Maybe you brought out the creativity in me."

As Grandma drove Emma home, Emma thought that perhaps her grandmother was more creative than either of them realized. She just needed a little encouragement.

Abby had been invited to spend the night at Bryn's house on Saturday. Shortly after she got there, she confided to Bryn that she was worried about having the group dinner at her house. "My mom came down with the flu on Thursday," she explained. "She couldn't go to work yesterday and she never even made it out of bed today."

"We need to discuss this with the DG," Bryn said as she reached for her phone. Soon it was agreed that an emergency meeting was needed, and by 8:00 all five girls were at Bryn's home.

"As you all know, the dance is only six days away," Bryn reminded everyone. "We need to nail down some of the details for that night." She now explained Abby's problem with hosting the group dinner.

"Naturally, there's a chance my mom will be better by then," Abby told her friends. "But there's also a chance that she won't. Anyway, my dad suggested we have the dinner somewhere else."

"We could've had it here," Bryn said, "except that my mom's having bunko on Friday night."

"There's no way we can have it at my house," Emma told them. "Our dining room isn't even big enough for six people. No way could we have ten."

"I suppose we could have it at my house," Cassidy offered. "It's not nearly as nice as Bryn or Abby's, but our dining room is big enough."

"I have an idea," Abby said suddenly. "What if we skip the group dinner this time. That way it will be more mysterious when we go to the dance. Our blind dates will pick us up, we'll all ride in the limo together, and we won't find out who our dates are until we're at the dance." Abby's real reason for suggesting this was twofold. She *did* feel guilty for not being able to have the dinner like she'd offered a week ago. But more than that she hoped this would be a good way to spare Leonard from a miserable dinner if Devon threw a hissy fit when she discovered who her date really was. It would be easier to handle the mess at the masquerade ball with lots of other people around to absorb some of the crud. And if Abby was lucky, maybe Devon wouldn't even figure things out until after a few dances.

"But the group dinner was so fun last time," Emma reminded them. "I thought we all agreed that it was a good way to break the ice—"

"I like Abby's idea," Devon interrupted. "Think about it—our blind dates show up at our doors, we don't know who they are, we all ride together in the limo. It'll be fun."

"That's a great idea," Abby agreed eagerly.

"Except that if the guys come to our doors, they'll know who we are," Cassidy pointed out.

"How about if we meet somewhere else?" Devon suggested. "Or we could all be at the same house when the guys pick us up."

So they put it to the vote, and to Abby's relief, the majority agreed to forgo the group dinner and be picked up together. However, the majority was only three of them. Emma and Bryn were still uncertain about giving up the group dinner. But they discussed it a while longer, and eventually Emma and Bryn came around.

"So where do we meet?" Bryn asked. "Where will the guys pick us up?"

They discussed various options, but each one seemed to have some major flaw until Bryn suggested her grandparents' house. After they all agreed that could work, Bryn called her grandmother and, after explaining their dilemma, she received the green light. "Gram's really excited about it," Bryn told them as she hung up. "Grandpa will have his camcorder running, and Gram offered to put out some appetizers for us."

"That's great," Abby told her. "Your grandmother's a great cook."

Bryn suddenly remembered their last group date and how it was fun to gather afterward—their chance to discuss the evening and their individual dates. "Hey, what if we end it with a sleepover like we did for the homecoming dance?" she asked. "A chance for us girls to regroup and dish about our dates."

"That sounds good," Emma agreed. "And we can rate our dates again."

"But where will we have it?" Devon asked.

"Why not here?" Bryn suggested.

"What about your mom's bunko?" Abby asked.

"Oh, the ladies will be long gone by then." Bryn grinned. "Besides that, there'll be really good leftovers because Mom always makes way too much food for bunko night." Naturally that cinched the deal.

With that settled, Cassidy, Emma, and Devon left and it was just Bryn and Abby again. "You have to see the shoes I got to go with my dress," Bryn said as she went for the closet, removing a shiny black box. "Check these babies out." She opened it to show a glitzy pair of golden shoes with dainty straps and stocky heels.

"Pretty." Abby picked up a sleek shoe. But she noticed the price on the box and couldn't hide her shock. "Did you really pay that much for these?" She set the expensive shoe back in the tissue paper.

"Yeah. Plus shipping." Bryn nodded almost as if proud of this.

"Seriously?"

"Hey, I want to look hot."

"For shoes you'll only wear once?" Abby was trying to wrap her head around this. Even though her basketball shoes were not cheap, they wouldn't cost even one-third of what Bryn had plunked down for these. And Abby would wear her high-tops all season and probably even afterward.

Bryn laughed. "You sound like my dad now."

"Sorry." Abby didn't want to imagine what her own dad would say if she spent that kind of money on something she'd wear one time.

Now Bryn went over to her dresser to pick up a glittering piece of jewelry. "Look at this headpiece." She slid it over her shiny blonde hair. "Isn't it fabulous?"

"Very pretty." Abby forced a congenial smile. No need to rain on Bryn's parade.

"I know what you're thinking." Bryn removed the headpiece and set it down.

"What?" Abby sat down on Bryn's bed.

"That I'm over the top. I'm spending too much money. Obsessing over fashion." She grinned. "But you know me—fashion is my passion."

"I know . . . but it seems like you could be fashionable without sending your family to the poorhouse."

Bryn laughed. "Now you really sound like Dad."

"Sorry." Abby shrugged. "I guess I'm just a practical person."

"The thing is, I had to pull out all the stops—I have to one-up Devon."

Abby frowned. "Why?"

"*Why?*" Bryn was pacing across her room now, as if she were frustrated. "Because she stole Tara's Juliet dress."

"She didn't steal it, Bryn. She rented it."

"Yeah, yeah . . . That's what she says. But I should've gotten that dress. And I have a feeling she knew that."

"How would she know that?"

Bryn held up her hands. "I don't know. All I know is that I have to look hotter than Devon at this dance. And I'm doing everything I can to make sure I do."

"Well, your dress is beautiful. At least it will be when it's finished. And the shoes and headpiece are gorgeous." Abby smiled. "So I'm guessing you've got this one in the bag."

"Really?"

Abby cringed to imagine how Devon would react when she discovered that Leonard was her blind date. She could throw a very ugly fit, or she might even refuse to go to the dance. "Yeah, I think so."

"What's bugging you?" Bryn asked curiously. "You don't seem like yourself, Abby. You haven't for the last week. What's up?"

"Nothing."

"Worried about who's taking you to the dance?"

"Not really." Abby looked evenly at her. "I actually wouldn't care if I was set up with the lamest, geekiest boy in the school."

"Really?" Bryn looked skeptical.

"Really."

Bryn studied Abby, rubbing her chin thoughtfully. "I wish I could put you to the test."

Abby stared at her supposedly best friend. "You mean if you were picking my blind date, you'd choose a geeky guy?"

"Maybe so. Just to see if you really meant that."

Abby frowned at her. "So did you set me up?"

"You know I can't tell you that."

"Well, even if you did, and even if you picked a total geek, I would not care."

Bryn laughed. "Well, you are definitely a bigger woman than I am."

Abby wanted to argue this point, but she was tired of talking about blind dates and geeks. And she was tired of thinking about it too. The sooner this dance came and went, the happier she would be.

• • ● • •

Abby had promised to make it home in time to go to church with her parents, but because her mom was still under the weather, Abby and Dad went to church without her. And afterward, to give Mom some more undisturbed resting time, Dad suggested they go out for lunch.

"What'd you think of today's sermon?" Dad asked after the waitress took their order.

Abby tried to remember the theme of the sermon. It wasn't that she hadn't been listening, exactly . . . although her mind might've been wandering a little. "It was good," she said slowly, trying to recall what was said.

Dad chuckled. "Meaning you can't remember?"

"I just went kinda blank," Abby confessed. "Oh, yeah, I remember. It was about being a light in a dark world."

"That's right." Dad nodded. "So what about the sermon stood out to you, Abby? Tell me how you can apply the teaching to your own life."

She knew that Dad couldn't help acting like a teacher. That was just who he was. And she knew the easiest way to get beyond this was to play along—and then change the subject. So she thought hard. "I guess the part about being a light to my friends," she said.

"That's great," he said. "Do you feel like you're a light to your friends?"

She shrugged, fingering the paper napkin. "I try to be."

"I realize peer pressure—even in a Christian school—can be tough when you're a teen," he said gently.

"Yeah. Just because Northwood is a Christian school does not mean all the kids there are Christians, Dad. For sure."

"So you probably get lots of opportunities to be a light then."

"I guess so." She took a sip of ice water, trying to think of a new conversation topic.

"Because I know how it goes with friends," he continued. "You either influence them or they influence you. Right?"

She nodded. "Yeah . . . I suppose that's mostly right."

"So which are you, Abby?"

"Huh?"

"An influencer? Or the one who's being influenced?"

She frowned. "I don't know. Probably both . . . I mean, sometimes."

"Because you really should be the influencer."

She resisted the urge to roll her eyes. She knew Dad hated that. But really, was he that clueless?

"I know it's not easy, honey. But you need to believe in yourself—and you need to believe that God is at work in you. And when you do that, you can take the leadership role with your friends."

"Some of my friends don't like being led, Dad."

"But that sounds like they want to do the leading . . . and what happens if they want to lead where you shouldn't go?"

"Then I don't go there."

He studied her closely.

"Don't worry," she assured him. "I don't let my friends pressure me into things I don't want to do, Dad."

"It's important to understand how the company you keep can influence you, Abby."

She frowned. "What do you mean?"

"I mean sometimes kids think their friends are a neutral influence. But most of the time that's not true. Your friends can influence you even when you don't know it. The company you keep is a major influence on who you are, Abby. On who you become."

Abby knew her dad meant well, but sometimes he just didn't get it. For instance, if he had any idea what Devon was really like, well, he would certainly disapprove of this wild friend. He might even insist that Abby discontinue associating with her. And yet Devon actually had very little influence on Abby. At least Abby didn't think she did. However, Abby was aware that she'd been fretting over Devon quite a bit lately. Not about Devon's "influence" but about how furious Devon would be when she discovered that Abby had set her up with Leonard Mansfield for her blind date. But was Abby going to confide about that to her dad? She didn't think so.

Dad continued his mini-lecture about friends and the company you keep until the waitress brought their food. And then Abby deftly changed the subject to sports. "Basketball season starts in a couple of weeks." She reminded him that she needed new high-tops. "And did I tell you that Belinda Matthews grew a couple of inches? So I won't have to play center this year. It looks like we'll have a pretty good team."

To her relief, Dad took the bait and for the rest of their meal, they talked primarily about sports. Of course, her dad's words continued to ring in her head. She knew that there was a sliver of truth in his warning about the influence of friends. But she also knew she was a strong person. And she would never let someone like Devon take her where she didn't want to go. However, she was concerned about Devon's influence over her best friend. Bryn seemed to be acting more and more like Devon. Not that Bryn was boy crazy exactly. But she seemed to be getting shallower . . . and snootier too. What if Devon's influence was changing Bryn?

As Dad drove them home, Abby thought about Devon's upcoming date with Leonard—she knew beyond any shadow of a doubt that Devon would think he was a geek. And at one point, Abby had nearly decided to switch dates with Devon and go out with Leonard herself. That would be preferable to having Devon hurt his feelings. But maybe Devon needed to spend an evening with someone like Leonard. Maybe it would be a good way to remind Devon that geeks were people too—that they had feelings. And it might also be a good way for Devon to show her true colors to someone like Bryn. Even if Bryn was shallow sometimes, she had never been intentionally mean. At least she never used to be. And Abby felt certain that if Bryn observed Devon treating someone like Leonard badly, Bryn might rethink her relationship with Devon. Bryn might realize that Devon truly was a bad influence.

By the time they got home, Abby had made up her mind. No matter what went down this week, she was not going to be intimidated by the potential of Devon's wrath. She was not going to undo Devon's blind date. Devon's Romeo would be played by Leonard.

Of course, Abby would have to do whatever she could to prepare Leonard for his big night. She would do everything possible to ensure that his costume looked great and that his evening was a success. Not that it actually seemed possible. But if Devon threw a hissy fit, which was highly likely, Abby would go out of her way to make sure that Leonard wasn't too badly hurt. She would dance with him herself as well as entice the other DG members to take turns. She would go out of her way to make the event go smoothly. And she would also be prepared to do whatever was necessary to repair things with Leonard afterward. Which she knew was likely. Somehow, someway, she would make sure that this thing ended well for Leonard.

She felt fairly sure that her dad wouldn't approve of what she'd done or how she was handling it, but it wasn't like he really needed to know all the dirty details. Still, she reassured herself, maybe this could be her way of being a light in a dark place . . . being an influence. She could only hope.

Even though Cassidy had completed all the machine-stitching on her Dorothy costume at Bryn's grandmother's house, she still had lots of hand-sewing to finish. Thankfully, Emma had offered to help her. And on Wednesday after school, the two of them sat together in Cassidy's room . . . sewing.

"With all this sewing, I kinda feel like I've gone back in time," Emma said as she threaded a needle. "Like I'm really becoming Emma Woodhouse and living inside a Jane Austen book."

"I know what you mean. I can't believe I made this costume—and I'd never even threaded a needle before." Cassidy held up the gingham dress where she'd just pinned up the hem. "I mean, I realize it wasn't a real complicated garment to make. At least that's what Bryn's grandma said when she was helping me, but the fact I made it myself is pretty cool. My parents were totally impressed."

"I'm impressed too," Emma told her. "Didn't know you had it in you."

"That's because you're the creative one," Cassidy reminded her. "By the way, I can't wait to see how your bonnet turned out. Or how you'll look as Emma."

"I think my costume looks pretty authentic if I do say so myself." Emma smiled contentedly as she sewed on the blouse. "But I still wonder what my Mr. Knightley will be wearing."

"Don't you wonder *who* your Mr. Knightley will be?"

"I'm trying not to think about that too much," Emma admitted.

"Yeah, me too." Cassidy let out a long sigh. "I'm so tired of Bryn and Devon acting like their lives might fall apart if they don't land the perfect dates. It makes me wish we'd never started this silly blind date thing in the first place."

"Not me. I'm glad we did it. I have absolutely no regrets."

Cassidy accidentally stuck her finger with the sharp needle and let out a loud yelp.

"What?" Emma looked up from her sewing. "You have regrets?"

Sucking on her pricked finger, Cassidy slowly shook her head. Okay, the truth was she *did* have regrets. Huge and serious regrets that she had to keep completely to herself. She knew beyond any shadow of a doubt that she never should've gotten Darrell Zuckerman for Bryn's date. Sure, she'd been irritated with Bryn at the time. And to be fair, Bryn had been acting like a spoiled prima donna that day. But Cassidy had been wrong, wrong, wrong to set Bryn up with Darrell. And Cassidy knew that it was going to come back to haunt her. In fact, it was already haunting her.

As she hemmed the skirt of the jumper part of the dress

she remembered how helpful and sweet Bryn's grandmother had been on Saturday. And it had been very generous of Bryn to invite all of the DG members over there to work on their costumes together. Then, like salt to the wound, Bryn had actually been surprisingly nice to Cassidy these past couple of days. So much so that Cassidy had been tempted to pick a fight with Bryn at lunch today. As if quarrelling would make things better! How stupid was that?

But it was too late. What was done was done. Bryn's Jay Gatsby would be geeky Darrell Zuckerman and there was nothing Cassidy could do about it. Not without garnering the wrath of both Darrell and Bryn. And even though Bryn would probably make a huge stink on Friday night, Cassidy had good reason to be more worried about Darrell than Bryn. She wished she could tell Emma about all of this, but she knew that would be breaking the rules. Until the big night, mum was the word. And maybe that was for the best. Cassidy had a feeling that if she was allowed to speak about this, her floodgates would be opened and she'd never get them closed again.

"I can tell something's bugging you," Emma said urgently. "Want to talk about it?"

"Of course, I *want* to talk about it," Cassidy snapped. "But I *can't*. Remember, this stupid blind date stuff is *top secret*."

"Oh . . . well, okay then."

"I'll probably get an ulcer from all this. They say stress is a killer."

"Wow, you're really having a hard time, aren't you?"

Cassidy grimaced in silence, focusing on her stitches. She should've just kept her mouth shut.

"That's too bad," Emma said. "The masquerade ball is

supposed to be enjoyable. I know I've been having a lot of fun preparing for it."

"It's been partly fun," Cassidy confessed. "It's just that I'm not looking forward to Friday. Not at all."

"I know this has to do with whoever you set up."

"Duh."

"I wish I knew who it is," Emma said quietly. "I know it's not me."

Cassidy kept her eyes on her sewing. No way was she going to spill the beans. It was bad enough she'd made a mess of things. It would only get worse if she was the one girl in the DG unable to keep a secret.

"Hmm," Emma murmured. "And since I know which girl I set up, well, I feel pretty certain that it's either Bryn or Devon."

Cassidy looked up. "How'd you figure that out?"

"Simple deduction."

"Yeah, well, you still don't know for sure. And at least I didn't tell you."

"And that actually makes a lot of sense."

"What makes sense?"

"That you're feeling worried."

"Why?" Cassidy paused from pulling the needle through the fabric.

"Because Bryn and Devon both have such high expectations for their dates. And I'm guessing that you got one of them a dud. Right?"

Cassidy moaned. "You didn't hear that from me."

"Well, I wouldn't admit this to anyone else," Emma said slowly, "but if it turns out that you set Devon up with a loser, I'd say she might just deserve it. She's been so full of herself lately I can hardly stand her. I know it's partly because of what's going on with her mom at home, but, hey, we all have problems. You don't have to be a witch about it. So, really, if you stuck it to Devon . . . good for you." Emma chuckled.

Cassidy frowned. She did not feel the least bit reassured by this.

"Oh no," Emma said quietly.

"*What?*" Cassidy looked at Emma. She was pulling the needle through the white blouse with a shocked expression.

"Oh no!" Emma shook her head.

"Did you make a sewing mistake? Did you sew the sleeve closed?"

"No. I figured it out, Cass. You set *Bryn* up with a loser, didn't you? And now you wish you hadn't. Am I right? *Or am I right?*"

Cassidy knew there was no point denying this as she locked eyes with Emma. "I wish I could undo it. I would give anything to undo it."

"Oh, my goodness!" Emma looked truly horrified. "And Bryn has gone to so much work to make her costume absolutely perfect. She's been so certain that her date is going to be Mr. Wonderful—and that he's going to be impeccably dressed as the great Jay Gatsby, and they are going to be the most stunning couple at the dance. Oh, Cassidy—this is awful!"

"I know."

"Why would you do that to her? Of all the girls in the school—Bryn could probably have had her choice of almost any guy. Why would you purposely get her a dud?"

"I don't know why I did it, Emma." Cassidy felt close to tears. "But there's no way to get out of it now. I mean, if I could gently let him down and find someone else for Bryn, I would. But this guy—the one I set Bryn up with—well, he's sworn he'll get even with me if the date goes sideways. And it will go sideways. I just know it will. And then I'm toast."

"Oh, Cass, what are you going to do?"

"I've imagined all kinds of escape scenarios. Like getting sick on Friday morning and not even going to school. Or leaving the country."

"I mean seriously, Cass. What are you going to do?"

"I think my best option might be to offer to trade dates with Bryn."

"Except that would leave the elegant Daisy Buchanan dancing with a scruffy scarecrow."

"I know." She sighed loudly. "Believe me, I know."

"I could trade my date with her," Emma offered. "Mr. Knightley should be somewhat elegant looking. He might be able to pass as Bryn's Gatsby."

"But what if your date is a dud too?" Cassidy asked.

"Oh." Emma shrugged. "I guess that's possible. Hey, maybe we'll all have duds. And if we do, then no one should complain, right?"

"Wouldn't that be great," Cassidy said with relief. "How cool would it be if everyone has gotten everyone a lame date? Then I won't stand out as the girl who blew it."

"Actually, that's not possible," Emma admitted. "I got a *good* blind date for, well, I can't say who I got him for. But I know she'll be happy with him."

"Do you think that *he'd* want to trade?"

Emma frowned. "But he'd have on the wrong costume too."

"Yeah, yeah . . . I know. It's a mess. A total mess. And it's all my fault. I can't believe how stupid I was. What I wouldn't do for a do-over."

"Maybe the guy will get sick. I heard the flu is going around. Maybe you should have someone waiting in the wings—just in case your guy gets sick."

"Yeah . . . right," Cassidy said with no enthusiasm. "Hopefully I'll get sick. I should go hang at Abby's house to see if I can contract her mom's flu bug. That would be nice."

"Poor Cass."

"Don't you mean poor Bryn?"

"Yeah, but I didn't want to make you feel worse." Emma shook out the white blouse. "Look, this is all done. You're going to make such a cute Dorothy. I can just imagine you with your brown braids tied in red ribbons and your ruby slippers."

"You mean if I don't come down with the flu."

Emma ignored that. "What about Toto?" she asked.

"Huh?"

"You need a Toto doggy, Cass."

"I think I might need a guard dog more."

"You should carry your Toto in a basket like in the movie. I used to have a stuffed black Scotty dog. I might even be able to find him in the attic. That is, if you're interested. His name was McDuffy and he was very sweet. Want to borrow him? I might even have a basket you could use."

"Sure," Cassidy said glumly. "Make it a good solid basket in case I need to defend myself. On second thought, maybe I can borrow Abby's bow and arrow."

"Oh, Cass." Emma hung the finished blouse on the hanger. "You're obsessing over this. Blowing it all out of proportion."

"I think I'm just being realistic." Cassidy finished the last stitch on the dress's hem.

"Instead of freaking, you should be praying."

"You don't think I have?" She knotted the thread and bit it off with her teeth.

"So if you prayed about it, why are you still so worried?"

"Huh?" Cassidy smoothed out the blue-and-white gingham skirt.

"Jesus said to pray about things instead of worrying. Remember?"

"Uh-huh." Cassidy hung the jumper over the white blouse, admiring how nice it looked together.

"And don't forget that God promises to bring good out of bad, Cass. Remember that verse? If you love God and are called according to his purposes, he turns something bad into something good. That's not an exact translation, but it's close. I'll bet that God can bring something good out of your mess too."

"Yeah, I know that Bible verse too. Problem is that when I asked, uh, that certain guy . . . well, I'm not sure I was called *according to God's purposes*—if you know what I mean. I think I was more called according to my own selfish and vengeful purposes. How can God make that into good?"

"Because God is gracious. Everyone makes mistakes, Cass." Emma stood, reaching for her coat. "But God always forgives."

"I know God forgives, but I'm not so sure about Bryn—not to mention a certain merciless guy who has already promised to make my life miserable."

"Tell you what." Emma zipped her coat. "I'll be praying about this situation a lot now. You're not alone."

"Thanks. But please, do not mention it to anyone. Besides God that is."

"You know you can trust me." Emma hugged her. "And don't worry so much, okay?"

"I'll try." Cassidy felt a smidgeon better now. "Thanks, Em. It helps knowing that you know. At least you'll be able to explain to my parents what happened to . . . you know, regarding my premature demise at the masquerade ball."

"Oh, Cass!" Emma laughed. "You can be such a drama queen sometimes."

Cassidy walked Emma to the front door. "I feel like my days are numbered," she said. "Like it'll all be over on Friday night."

"One way or another it will." Emma hugged her again. "Promise me that you won't keep obsessing over this. It's not doing anyone—especially you—any good. You need to pray about it, Cass. Trust God to take care of it for you. Okay?"

"I'll try," Cassidy promised.

"Besides, like you mentioned, worrying that much is bad for your health. It can make a person physically ill," Emma reminded her as she went out the door.

As Cassidy waved good-bye, she wondered if that was really true. Could she actually make herself sick with worry? And if so, could she possibly do it by Friday?

Devon had gone out of her way to be super sweet to Bryn all day on Thursday. She'd complimented her outfit a couple of times, and she'd pointed out how great Bryn's hair looked during lunch. If it wouldn't look totally hokey, Devon would probably even offer to carry Bryn's books . . . or shine her shoes . . . or wipe her nose. Somehow she needed to win Bryn over completely. Because she needed Bryn's help. Well, she needed Bryn's *grandmother's* help.

"I have a problem with my costume," Devon confided to Bryn as they walked toward the school parking lot at the end of the day. Devon had been so nice to Bryn that she'd actually earned herself a ride home in Bryn's car. "I don't know what I'm going to do."

"What kind of problem?" Bryn asked with a slightly suspicious expression.

"Well, I tried it on last night—just to get the full effect, you know. And when I bent over to put on my shoes, the zipper broke."

"Oh?" Bryn reached into her purse for her keys. "Can't you fix it?"

"I tried and tried to fix it." Devon frowned. "I think I made it worse."

Bryn clicked her key to unlock the car. "So what are you going to do?"

"I called an alterations place," Devon explained as they got into the car, "and they said they can't get to it until next week."

"And that will be too late." Bryn sounded slightly haughty as she turned the key in the ignition.

"Do you think your grandmother might be able to help me?" Devon asked hopefully.

Bryn turned to look evenly at Devon. "I don't know."

"I could pay her," Devon offered helplessly.

Now Bryn smiled—in that sort of superior way. "Oh, my grandmother would never accept money for helping someone."

"But do you think she would help me?"

Bryn opened her purse and pulled out her phone. "Why don't I give her a jingle for you."

"Thank you," Devon said eagerly. "I'll be forever in your debt."

Bryn laughed as she held the phone up to her ear. "Hey, Gram," she said lightly. "My friend Devon has experienced a small wardrobe malfunction. Apparently she tried to squeeze herself into the beautiful Juliet gown—you know, the one you sewed for Tara," Bryn said in a haughty tone. "Anyway, it split wide open and now she needs help fixing it."

Devon tried to hide her irritation as she listened. Maybe this was called eating humble pie. But when she walked into the masquerade ball looking absolutely gorgeous as Juliet, it would be worth it.

"So you're not too busy." Bryn listened to the phone, slyly winking at Devon like she knew she had the upper hand. "Thanks, Gram. We'll go pick up the dress and be right over." She dropped her phone back into her purse, then turned to Devon. "Looks like we're good to go."

"Thank you so much!" Devon gushed. "And you don't need to stop by my house." She opened her oversized bag and extracted the Juliet dress. "I have it with me."

"You were feeling pretty confident, weren't you?"

"More like desperate," Devon confessed.

"What would you have done if Gram couldn't help you?" Bryn asked.

"I thought about using a bunch of safety pins to close it up," Devon admitted. "I was going to ask Emma to help pin me into the dress."

Bryn wrinkled her nose. "A bunch of safety pins? That doesn't sound terribly attractive. And what if a pin broke open during the dance?"

"Yeah, that might hurt."

"Sounds like the Juliet dress might be too small for you," Bryn said as she drove.

"Yeah, well, it was a bit snug on top," Devon confessed. "But I thought I'd lose a couple of pounds by the dance."

"Which is tomorrow."

"So . . . I wonder if your grandma could let it out a little."

"Maybe it wasn't such a great idea to go as Juliet after all."

Devon could hear the smugness in Bryn's tone. And she

knew that Bryn had the advantage here. Perhaps the best way to play this was to grovel a little. "You're probably right," Devon said contritely. "Maybe this is fate's way of paying me back for snagging the Juliet dress. But honestly, Bryn, I had no idea that it had been worn by your sister or that your grandmother had made it when I picked it out."

"Yes . . . but you knew afterward, Devon. I told you. Remember?"

"Yeah, that's true. I guess I was just being greedy. I'd fallen in love with the dress, and I really wanted to be Juliet." Devon looked at Bryn's perfect profile. "I'm sorry," she said quietly. "I guess that was pretty selfish, huh?"

Bryn nodded.

"But your Gatsby dress is absolutely gorgeous," Devon told her. "And you'll look fabulous as Daisy." Now Devon got an idea—and it wasn't a bad one either. "But if you really want to be Juliet, I'm willing to trade dresses with you, Bryn. I can see now that it was wrong for me to glom onto the Juliet dress like I did. I mean, after all, it was kind of in your family."

"That's true."

"So if you want to trade . . . I'd be willing." The truth was Devon was more than just willing. She'd been trying not to drool over Bryn's beautiful golden-girl dress with its low-cut neckline and all those sparkling beads. She'd love to wear it to the dance.

"Well, if we traded costumes then we'd have to trade our blind dates too," Bryn reminded her. "Or else our costumes wouldn't match our dates."

"That's true." Devon frowned. "But since they're blind dates, maybe it wouldn't matter if we traded."

"Unless your date was a total loser," Bryn pointed out.

"What if *your* date was the loser?"

"No way! Jay Gatsby cannot be a loser."

"You think Romeo could be a loser?" Devon challenged.

Now they both started teasing and joking, and by the time they reached Bryn's grandparents' house they were both laughing. They were still laughing when they went inside.

"Sounds like you girls are having a good time," Bryn's grandmother said as she led them down to the basement.

"We were just speculating about our blind dates," Devon said as she handed Mrs. Jacobs the Juliet dress. "If they turn out to be total losers, Bryn and I are going on the warpath."

"The warpath?" Mrs. Jacobs frowned as she put on her glasses.

"Actually it will be more like the manhunt," Bryn clarified. "We decided we'll hunt down the best-looking guys and entice them to dance with us."

"Yeah, even if the guys turn out to be our friends' dates," Devon added.

"But how will that make your friends feel? Or your dates for that matter?" Mrs. Jacobs tipped her head to one side as she spread the Juliet dress out onto a cutting table.

"Well, if our dates turn out to be losers, it means our friends let us down," Bryn explained.

"And with friends like that who needs enemies?" Devon winked at Bryn. "Our friends would deserve to have their dates stolen from them."

"That doesn't sound like very good manners to me." Mrs. Jacobs looked at Bryn. "I thought my granddaughter was brought up to be more courteous than that."

"Oh, Gram." Bryn grinned. "We're only kidding."

"Sort of," Devon said quietly.

"Anyway, our friends wouldn't *really* set us up with losers," Bryn said with confidence.

"How do you define *loser*?" Mrs. Jacobs examined the back of the Juliet dress.

"You know, it's a geeky, nerdy sort of guy," Devon told her. "They must've had guys like that back in your day."

Bryn tossed Devon what seemed like a warning look.

"Hmm . . ." Mrs. Jacobs reached for a little tool. "I'm sure that some people thought my Stanley was like that."

"Grandpa?" Bryn looked surprised. "You're saying that Grandpa was a geek?"

"Define *geek*," her grandmother said.

Bryn looked at Devon.

"You know . . . kinda nerdy . . . social misfit . . . uh, loser," Devon said cautiously.

Mrs. Jacobs made a funny smile. "Well, that's probably how some kids saw Stanley back in high school."

"But Grandpa's not like that at all," Bryn said defensively.

"You didn't know your grandfather in high school." Mrs. Jacobs handed Devon the sharp tool and showed her how to pick out the threads to remove the zipper. "But I'll tell you girls this much. Some of the boys you call geeks or nerds right now will probably end up being much more successful than some of the high school boys you currently admire. Trust me, everything changes as you get older." She chuckled as she went over to a cabinet. "Let me see if I can find a zipper the right length and color."

As Devon worked to cut the threads holding the broken zipper in place, she thought about the date she'd set up for Cassidy. Even though Russell was new to school and Devon didn't really know him, she would have to describe him as pretty nerdy. He looked like a geek, talked like a geek. He probably even walked like a geek. But if Bryn's grandmother was right, maybe Russell wasn't so bad after all. Devon felt somewhat reassured.

She'd been feeling slightly guilty to think of how disappointed Cassidy might be when she discovered that Devon had set her up with a geek. Especially since Cassidy had been acting pretty decent to Devon lately. Just today Cass had gone out of her way to help Devon with her civics assignment, showing her some good websites and even letting Devon borrow her iPad during lunch. It was almost like Cassidy was really trying to be a good friend. Well, if Mrs. Jacobs was right, Devon had done Cass a favor by setting her up with a geek. At least that's what she was telling herself now.

Devon had just finished removing the broken zipper when Bryn told her grandmother that the Juliet dress also needed to be let out as well. "Otherwise, Devon will probably bust out another zipper," Bryn said teasingly.

"Well, I made the dress with plenty of room for alterations," Mrs. Jacobs told them. "When you put that much time and energy into a drama costume, you hope that it will get well used. Although I'm a bit surprised that the drama department is allowing you to wear it to a dance." She frowned as she reached for the gown.

As Devon watched Mrs. Jacobs opening up some seams inside the dress, she explained her idea to rent wardrobe items. "All the money goes directly to the drama department's costume budget," she said.

"That was a clever suggestion, Devon." Mrs. Jacobs shook out the dress. "Now let's try this on you and see if we can make it fit you more comfortably."

As Mrs. Jacobs was fitting the dress onto Devon, Bryn went upstairs to talk to her grandpa and look for something to eat.

"You're a very pretty girl," Mrs. Jacobs told Devon as she pinned the sides of the dress back together. "And you look very pretty in this gown."

"Thanks." Devon smiled with satisfaction.

"But like I tell my own granddaughter, *pretty is as pretty does*."

"I've heard that before." Devon frowned. "Although I'm not totally sure about what it means, exactly."

"It means that you are only as pretty as your actions. If a pretty girl acts out in unattractive ways, she will become unattractive." Mrs. Jacobs peered over the top of her reading glasses, as if to see whether Devon grasped this.

"Yeah, I thought it was something like that."

"So many young people focus too much on their outward appearance. Sometimes I fear they neglect their interior appearance." She stepped back to look at the dress. "I've pointed this out to Bryn a number of times but, like you, she's young. I'm afraid she hasn't quite figured these things out yet."

"I guess we're both still working on it." Devon tried to sound reassuring.

"Well, you seem like a smart girl to me." Mrs. Jacobs carefully lifted the dress over Devon's head and took it over to a sewing machine where she sat down. "I hope that you make smart choices too."

"I'm not exactly sure what you mean." Devon pulled her clothes back on and went over to watch Mrs. Jacobs sewing the dress. "Choices about what?"

"I mean that I hope both you and Bryn will choose to be gracious and kind to your blind dates—no matter what kind of boys you assume they are. I hope that you girls will choose to be courteous and do all that you can to make the evening an enjoyable one for everyone."

"Oh . . ." Devon slowly nodded. "Well, we were just joking about our blind dates. Besides, I'm sure they'll be perfectly nice guys and we'll all probably have a good time."

Bryn came into the room with a bag of microwave popcorn in hand. "I'd offer to share it with you," she teased Devon, "except that I know how you're watching your weight so you don't bust out your zipper again."

"Your grandmother is making the dress big enough that I don't have to." Devon reached into the bag and pulled out a handful of popcorn.

"Yes, and I was also giving Devon the *pretty is as pretty does* lecture," Mrs. Jacobs said over her shoulder.

"Oh, dear." Bryn frowned. "Sorry about that," she said quietly to Devon.

"Bryn," Mrs. Jacobs said in a warning tone.

"Just kidding, Gram." Bryn giggled. "But lecturing my friends?"

"I lecture you sometimes, don't I?"

"Yes, but—"

"And you know that I love you, don't you?"

"Yes, but—"

"Here's another old saying." She looked up from her sewing. "A word to the wise is sufficient."

Bryn grinned at Devon. "I get that one a lot from her."

"What's it mean?"

"It means that if we're smart, we'll listen to her," Bryn teased.

"That's right," Mrs. Jacobs said as she returned to sewing.

Devon thought about Bryn's grandmother's words as she waited for her to finish fixing the dress. And when Devon thanked Mrs. Jacobs for helping her, she knew that she was partially thanking her for the unexpected little talk as well. Oh, she didn't want to say the words aloud and she didn't even like to admit it to herself—but she knew she needed to hear that. It was good, sound advice and she'd probably be smart to take it. The problem was that Devon was pretty sure she wouldn't.

After Gram's mini-lecture to Devon yesterday, Bryn was having second thoughts about having everyone meet up with their blind dates at her grandparents' house. Really, what had she been thinking? As Bryn carried her friends' overnight bags down to the basement—for the sleepover they'd be having afterward—she wished she'd thought to host the pre-party down here instead. Because, really, what if Gram and Grandpa decided to give everyone a little pep talk or reminded the guys about minding their manners or how ladies should be ladies or any of that stuff?

As she trudged back up the stairs, she knew it was too late to change things now. Gram was expecting them. Also, Bryn's dress was over there and she'd promised Gram that she'd come early to get ready there.

"All set?" Dad asked as Bryn came into the living room. "I think your mom's ready to kick us out now."

Bryn held up her big Dolce bag. "Hopefully, I've got everything I need."

Mom emerged from the kitchen. "I wish I didn't have to get the house ready for bunko or I'd go with you."

"That's okay." Bryn blew Mom a kiss. "Have fun with the ladies. We should be back here around midnight and I have my key." She glanced at Dad. "I'll try to keep everyone quiet until we get down to the basement."

"And I'll put the bunko leftovers in the fridge down there," Mom promised. "Have fun, sweetie!"

As Dad drove to her grandparents', Bryn felt fairly certain that she would have fun tonight. How could she not have fun wearing such a fabulous dress? She couldn't wait to see how everything looked all together now that the dress was completely finished.

"Make sure they get lots of photos," Dad said as he pulled up to his parents' two-story brick house.

"No problem." Bryn kissed him on the cheek and then hurried up to the front door. Gram had hung jack-o'-lantern lights around her front porch and about a dozen pumpkins were lined up along the steps leading to the door. Very welcoming and festive.

"Come in," Grandpa said, opening the door wide.

"Wow, it looks great in here," Bryn said as she noticed even more colorful Halloween decorations throughout the house. No one did holidays better than Gram. "And it smells good too." Maybe it wasn't a mistake to have the pre-party here after all.

"Gram's in the kitchen." He smacked his lips. "She's made some killer crab cakes and lots of other goodies for you and your friends. But for some reason she's banned me from any more sampling." He made a mock frown.

Bryn patted his cheek. "Hopefully you'll get some leftovers." She went into the kitchen just as Gram was setting cheese puffs onto a platter. "Mmm." Bryn reached for a hot cheese puff. "I better make sure these are okay."

Gram chuckled. "You and your grandpa."

"Yummy." Bryn kissed Gram's cheek. "And the house looks fabulous too. Thanks so much for doing this."

"Oh, I'm having fun," Gram assured her. "Makes me feel young. And I can't wait to see all your friends in their costumes."

"Speaking of costumes." Bryn glanced around the kitchen. "Where's my dress?"

"Up in the guest bedroom. I thought you could finish getting ready up there. And your girlfriends can use that room if they need to make any last-minute wardrobe adjustments too."

"Cool." Bryn snagged another cheese puff, then grabbed up her bag and hurried upstairs. Everything seemed to be working out just fine. And when she found her golden dress hanging in the closet, she couldn't have been happier. With every bead in place, it glittered and shimmered like something out of Hollywood. To think that Devon had actually suggested trading this dress for the old Juliet one. Ha! Bryn didn't mind that Devon assumed she was still miffed about the Juliet dress, but Bryn never would've given up this dress—no way!

She took the heavy garment off the hanger and carefully slipped it over her head. Naturally, it fit perfectly. She peered at her image in the mirror and smiled. It looked perfect too. She swayed from side to side, watching how the skirt moved so gracefully and elegantly, how the beading caught the light and glimmered. She could not wait to show this off on the dance floor tonight. And since she'd warned everyone in the

DG that she expected a blind date who could really dance, she fully expected that her friends would cooperate. Why wouldn't they?

She slipped into the expensive gold shoes, carefully fastening the straps and then checking them out in the mirror. More perfection. She'd already done her hair at home. Smoothing it back so it looked sleek and glossy, she had pinned it into place so that it resembled a flapper hairstyle. She'd actually considered cutting it, except she couldn't bear to part with her long hair. However, she'd cut a bit off the sides to make two perfect curls that went right alongside her cheeks. Now she picked up the glittering hair band that Gram had helped her make and slid it onto her head, using bobby pins to secure it. It too was perfect.

Bryn had studied the makeup from *The Great Gatsby* movie and did her best to imitate it. She was putting on a pair of fake diamond teardrop earrings when she heard a knock on the door. Abby quietly entered the room. "Your grandmother told me to come up." Abby's dark eyes grew big. "Wow, Bryn, you look gorgeous."

"Thanks." Bryn studied her image in the full-length mirror, trying to determine if any detail was missing.

"Seriously, you look even better than Carey Mulligan did in the movie," Abby assured her.

"Well, thank you very much." Bryn grinned.

"And since we just watched it, I know what I'm talking about." Abby made a face. "Although I still don't get why you'd want to imitate Daisy Buchanan. The woman was a mess, Bryn."

"A *tragic* mess," Bryn said in defense. Okay, the truth was Bryn had been caught off guard by the movie. She'd been so wrapped up in the glamour and costumes that she'd completely forgotten how violent and sad the story was. "And poor Daisy was caught in the middle of it. She was a tragic character."

"Caught in the middle? Tragic character?" Abby frowned. "Daisy was the cause of all the tragedy."

"How can you say that?"

"Think about it, Bryn. First Daisy breaks Gatsby's heart by marrying the rich dude—all because Gatsby is poor. Then she cheats on her rich husband to be with Gatsby because Gatsby suddenly has money. And then she's actually the hit-and-run driver who kills her husband's mistress. And finally, after Gatsby does all he can to win Daisy back, she goes back to her husband, who blames Gatsby for killing his mistress, and Gatsby gets shot—all because of selfish Daisy, who just heads off on her merry little way as if she did nothing wrong."

"Wow, someone is in a bad mood tonight." Bryn stared at Abby, trying to figure out why she was acting so grumpy.

"I'm just saying it like it was." Abby adjusted the strap on her quiver.

"Hopefully you don't plan to use your weapons on anyone tonight." Bryn paused to study Abby's costume. It was actually pretty authentic looking. "Cool jacket," she told her.

"Thanks. It was my mom's," Abby said in a slightly grumpy tone.

Bryn touched the side braid and smiled. "Nice touch. You really do look like Katniss. And you look like you're about to kick some serious—"

"Hello," Emma called out as she opened the bedroom door. "Your grandma said you guys would be up here."

"Look at you," Bryn gushed as Emma came into the room

dressed in a blue-and-white striped gown and wearing a broad-brimmed bonnet trimmed with pale blue ribbons. "You look so sweet. Just like something out of a Jane Austen film."

"That's the idea." Emma removed a dainty pair of white gloves. Then her eyes got wide as she stared at Bryn. "You look absolutely beautiful," she told her.

"Abby said I look even better than Carey Mulligan," Bryn bragged.

"Carey who?"

"From *The Great Gatsby* movie," Abby explained. "She played the notorious Daisy."

"Notorious?" Emma frowned.

"Never mind," Bryn said quickly. "Abby's in a bit of a snit for some mysterious reason. She wants to take it out on Daisy."

"Your costume is great," Emma told Abby. "It's really similar to the one in the movie. I love this jacket."

Bryn decided to attempt some congeniality. "And she even did the braid. But are you sorry you're wearing pants? Is that why you're a little out of sorts?"

"Not at all," Abby assured her. "And I'm not out of sorts." She sat down in the chair by the window, putting her feet up on the ottoman and her arms behind her head. "Unlike some people, I can actually relax in my outfit."

Bryn slipped a glittering bracelet onto her wrist. "You have a point there, Abs," she cheerfully admitted. "With all these beads, this dress isn't really designed for sitting."

"Well, you might regret that before the night is over," Abby said.

"What time is it?" Emma asked. "Shouldn't the others be here by now?"

"It's not even 7:00." Abby pointed to the alarm clock by the bed. "Lots of time. The guys won't be here until 7:30. Remember?"

"That's true." Bryn gave her hair one last spritz of hairspray. "But we still have to come up with a plan for how we're going to meet the guys."

This had been the big discussion at lunch today. It seemed everyone had a different idea of how this should be accomplished. Bryn thought all the girls should go downstairs together and meet their dates as a group. Because of their costumes, it would be obvious who went with who. Devon had partially agreed, but she wanted it to be even more casual than that. No coming down the staircase together—they would simply be mingling in the house when the guys arrived.

However, Cassidy had different ideas. She wanted them to meet their dates one by one, giving everyone a chance to actually visit with each other and to "acclimate," Cassidy had said—like they were all part of some unpredictable weather system. Abby had actually backed Cassidy's idea, except that she'd taken it a step further, suggesting that the couples should all go to different parts of the house for an allotted amount of time, before they all came back together for the limousine ride to the school. Emma had actually seemed to be leaning toward Bryn's direction, but because the lunch break ended, they never had a chance to put it to the vote. So they agreed to make the decision tonight—before the guys arrived at 7:30.

"Hey," Devon said as she entered the room with her head held high. Bryn blinked in surprise to see that Devon looked fabulous in the Juliet gown. Not only did the dress accentuate all of Devon's curves—and the girl certainly had them—but the rich jewel-tone colors really seemed to set off Devon's auburn hair, which was piled on top of her head in attractive, loose curls. She made a very romantic Juliet. Not that Bryn planned to tell her that.

"You look beautiful," Emma told Devon. "Very elegant."

"Your aunt did a great job on your hair," Bryn told her. "Very pretty."

"I hope my Romeo appreciates all this," Devon said as she stepped in front of Bryn to admire herself in the full-length mirror. She patted her curls. "At least I won't have to worry about keeping my hair straight and smooth tonight. Especially since it's starting to rain out there."

"You both look really glamorous," Emma told them. "I'm starting to feel pretty boring compared to you two."

"I think you look very pretty, Em," Abby called from where she was still sitting by the window. "And I'll bet you're more comfortable than either of them."

"That's probably true," Emma agreed as she sat primly on the edge of the bed, folding her hands in her lap.

Bryn laughed. "You don't just look like you're from a time gone by, you act like it too."

"Hey, I'm trying to get into character," Emma told her.

"Good idea," Bryn said. "We should all get into character before the guys get here."

There was a tap on the door and Bryn called out, "That better be you, Cassidy Banks!"

The door opened and "Dorothy" stepped into the room, sporting a wicker basket on her arm with a stuffed black Scotty nestled inside. "It's just me and my little dog too," Cassidy said.

They all gushed over her outfit and ruby-red shoes while

Cassidy examined their costumes. Finally Bryn clapped her hands. "Okay, people," she said loudly. "We need to make a decision here. How are we going to meet up with our blind dates?"

"I think we should all go downstairs and hang out until the guys get here and then just let whatever happens happen," Devon said. "No big deal."

"I want to make a motion," Cassidy said.

"Is this an official meeting?" Devon demanded.

"It is now," Cassidy declared. "And I move that we all meet our guys individually and we go with them to a separate part of the house, like Abby suggested at lunch. We can prearrange for who goes where. And then we all spend fifteen or twenty minutes alone with our blind date."

"I second that motion." Abby got up from the chair.

"All in favor?" Cassidy asked.

Abby and Cassidy and Emma all raised their hands.

"Opposed?" Cassidy asked.

Now Devon and Bryn raised their hands.

"The yeas have it," Cassidy announced.

"Yeah, we noticed." Bryn shrugged. "I don't really care *how* we do it. Mostly I just want to get this dress out on the dance floor ASAP. So I suggest we keep our little blind date meeting time to fifteen minutes. And grab your appetizers before then." She pointed to the clock by the bed. "That means we'll have until 7:45 to visit. Then we all come back to the living room for photos. And we should be in the limo before 8:00 and at the school a little after that. *Okay?*"

Abby made a mock salute. "Aye-aye, sir."

"Very funny." Bryn checked out her reflection in the mirror again. "I do not look the least bit like a sir, thank you very much." She turned back around and began assigning the girls to various parts of the house. Fortunately, her grandparents' home was large so there was plenty of space. "Don't forget about the appetizers," she reminded them. "I don't want Gram to feel bad." She looked at the clock again. "The guys should be here in about five minutes." She held a finger in the air. "I have a new idea. Let's all go down right now and get ourselves some food and then get settled in our various stations to wait. My grandpa will greet the guys and encourage them to get some food before he directs them to their separate spaces where we'll be waiting." She liked how this was shaping up. "I'll write down for him where to take the guys just in case he forgets." She smiled at her friends. "Does that work?"

They all agreed it was a good plan, but their expressions were completely different. With her arms folded across her front, Emma looked slightly impatient. Meanwhile, Cassidy was pacing back and forth as if she was seriously worried. Abby looked just plain unhappy. And Devon, with a creased brow, seemed somewhat irritated.

"Okay," Bryn told them. "Let's go down and get this party started. And, oh yeah, don't forget to put on your eye masks. They're all down by the front door."

As Bryn led the entourage down the stairs, she wondered who would be playing her Great Gatsby tonight. She had several guys in mind, and any one of them would look great as Jay.

"There you all are," Gram said as they came into the dining room. Then both Bryn's grandparents admired the costumes and even took some candid photos as the girls filled plates with appetizers.

Meanwhile Bryn explained the plan to Grandpa. "Let's see . . . Dorothy will be in the sunroom. Take the scarecrow to her."

"Dorothy and the scarecrow in the sunroom."

"Emma in the library with Mr. Knightley."

"This is kind of like playing Clue," he teased as he wrote. "Will Emma have a lead pipe or a wrench by any chance?"

"No." Bryn laughed. "But Katniss aka Abby has a bow and arrows. She'll be in the basement with Peeta."

"Got it," he said.

"Juliet in Gram's parlor with Romeo. And I'll be in the pool room."

"Maybe you should say the *billiards* room." He winked. "Doesn't that sound more appropriate for *The Great Gatsby*?"

"You're right." She adjusted her beaded headdress.

He grinned as he tucked the note into his pocket and picked up his camcorder. "I'll get as much footage as I can," he promised. "Maybe you'll want to post it on one of those facetube websites."

She laughed. "You mean YouTube. Or maybe Facebook." Then with her eye mask in place, Bryn carried her plate of food and a cup of punch to the pool/billiards room and prepared to wait. She really wasn't nervous. She knew she looked awesome. She knew that whoever her date was would think she looked awesome too. Mostly she just wanted to get on with it. She rolled the cue ball across the table, bouncing it off the bumper again and again.

"Hello?" She turned to see a guy wearing a black suit entering the room. "I'm Jay Gatsby," he said in a slightly nervous voice. Beneath his classic black jacket he had on a crisp white shirt and a neat black bow tie. Very Gatsby-like. However,

he wasn't very tall. She estimated that he was barely as tall as she was in these not-so-high heels. But he did have a nice firm chin.

She smiled and held out her hand. "I'm Daisy Buchanan," she said in a sweet voice, trying to add just a touch of a southern accent since Daisy was from Kentucky. "It's a pleasure to meet you, Jay." She studied him closely as he took her hand in his. He had a strong grasp and he seemed slightly familiar, but with the eye mask on, she couldn't be sure who he was. However, the brown hair, which was combed smoothly back, seemed vaguely familiar.

"Pleased to meet you, Daisy." He smiled as if he meant it. "You look very beautiful tonight."

"Thank you." She pointed at the plate in his hand. "I see you got yourself a little something to eat."

He nodded, his mouth twisting to one side as if he was about to speak and then decided differently. But something about that movement tickled some corner of her memory. This guy was definitely familiar. *But who was he?* She pointed to a wingback leather chair. "Care to sit?" she asked. "So you can eat."

"Thank you." He went over to the chair and then, as if unwilling to sit while she was still standing, he waited.

"Go ahead," she said. "I'd rather stand if you don't mind."

"Okay." He slowly sat, balancing the plate on his knees. "Thanks."

She watched him carefully as she strolled back and forth, running her hand along the polished wood of the pool table. He was definitely familiar to her. Even his voice sounded familiar. But she could not quite identify it. "I think we've met before," she said softly, trying to remain in character.

He nodded as he took a bite of crab cake. "Yes . . . I'm certain of it."

"So you recognize me?"

He nodded again, still chewing. "Yes . . . yes, I do." His mouth twisted to one side again—that same familiar gesture.

And that's when it hit her. "*Darrell Zuckerman?*" she exclaimed. In that same moment, she pulled off her eye mask and stared at her date in complete horror. "No way! Darrell Zuckerman? You're my blind date?"

He made an apologetic smile, then shrugged, slowly removing his eye mask. "You guessed it."

A wide gamut of emotions swept through her all at once. She felt seriously angry, outraged even. Who had done this to her? And in the next moment she felt slightly ashamed of herself. After all, Darrell was actually a pretty sweet guy—and a great lab partner in chemistry. *But a date?* That was absolutely nuts!

She was pacing again, trying to figure a way out of this mess.

"I'm sorry to disappoint you."

She turned around and glared at him. "Who did—" She paused, taking in a deep breath, trying to calm herself—even silently counting to ten. "Uh . . . I'm just curious . . . who set up the blind date?" she asked in a falsely sweet voice. "Which one of my friends?"

"Cassidy Banks."

"Ah . . ." She pressed her lips together, inwardly seething. "Dear, sweet Cassidy."

"I can see you're upset." He set his plate of food on a side table and slowly stood.

"I'm . . . just pretty shocked. That's all."

"I didn't know you were going to be my date, Bryn. If

I'd known you were who Cassidy was setting me up with, I would've said no right from the start."

She blinked in surprise. "You would've said *no*?"

"Absolutely." He nodded firmly.

"Seriously? You wouldn't have gone out with me if you'd known?" Now she felt indignant. Darrell Zuckerman was too good for her? It felt like the world was turning itself upside down. If this was supposed to be a joke, it was not funny.

"Hey, I might be a nerd, Bryn, but I'm not ignorant."

"Yes, Darrell, I'm well aware of that." She folded her arms across her front, controlling herself from really tearing into him as she spoke her mind.

"You're a nice girl and a good lab partner, but I know you never would've agreed to go out with me. Not of your own free will." He shoved his hands into his pants pockets, looking down at his feet as if he was embarrassed or maybe even angry. And really, he had every right to be angry. They both did. This was a mess. A tragic mess. Suddenly she remembered what Abby had said to her earlier—pointing out how selfish Daisy Buchanan had been, how she had ruined Jay Gatsby's life by being so shallow. Wasn't that exactly how Bryn was acting right now?

"I'm sorry, Darrell," she said quietly. "I honestly don't know what to say. I just felt kind of blindsided, you know?"

"Hey, I know exactly how you feel. This is seriously messed up. Cassidy *never* should've done this." He scowled darkly. "She's the one to blame."

Bryn could tell he was trying to act tough, but she could see that beneath his anger, he was hurt. Maybe even deeply hurt. And she knew it was her fault. "I'm sorry," she said again. "Really, I am."

"Forget about it." He nodded with a grim expression. "Anyway, I've had enough of this game. I think I should go." He started for the door.

"Wait, Darrell." She put her hand on his arm. "Please don't go."

He looked at her with a confused expression. "Why?"

"Because we have a date," she said with determination.

"Really?" He looked skeptical.

"Yes." She looked directly into his gray-blue eyes. "We do."

"Look, Bryn, I don't want a pity date from you. Understand?"

Now she remembered what Gram had said about Grandpa. And suddenly she saw Darrell through a different set of eyes. "This is *not* a pity date, Darrell." She gave him a genuine smile. "I swear to you, it's not. I want to go to the dance with you. I want you to be my Jay Gatsby."

He looked totally perplexed and still somewhat angry. "Are you sure about this?"

"I'm absolutely, positively sure."

"You're not punking me again?"

She shook her head no, then giggled. "I just have one teeny tiny little question, Darrell."

"What now?" He glowered at her.

"I know you're a genius, Darrell, but do you know how to dance?"

His stormy countenance broke into a crooked grin. "Do I know how to dance?"

"Yeah." She felt a surge of hope. "Do you?"

"My mom made me take dance lessons when I was in grade school," he confessed. "I hated it at first, but then it kind of grew on me." He chuckled. "And when I heard I was playing

Jay Gatsby, well, I even brushed up on the Charleston and a few other jazz-era dances."

"Seriously?" She could not believe her luck.

"Oh, yeah." He gave her a sassy wink. "I know how to cut a rug."

She glanced at the clock on the back wall, then linked her arm into his. "So, Jay, what are we waiting for?" They put their eye masks back on and went out to find how the others were faring.

12

Emma went to the library to wait for her blind date. She felt a little nervous as she nibbled at the appetizers Mrs. Jacobs had prepared for them, but Emma had already decided that no matter who her date was—whether he was a nerd, geek, jerk, jock, loser, dud, whatever—she was going to treat him with kindness and grace. Sort of like Emma Woodhouse would do—well, at least by the end of the book after Miss Woodhouse finally learned her lesson. Anyway, that was what Emma hoped and planned to do. She just wished that all the members of the DG would do the same. Keep your chin up, take the high road, keep a stiff upper lip—and all those other British idioms that sounded a bit silly if one wasn't a Brit.

As Emma sipped her punch and perused the bookshelves, she wondered how Bryn was doing with her blind date right now. Cassidy had never actually revealed who she'd set Bryn up with, but Emma knew that it had the makings of a disaster.

She also knew that if Bryn wanted to, she could not only make her blind date miserable, she could make all of them miserable. And so, just like she'd promised Cassidy—and like she'd been doing the past couple of days—Emma prayed. She specifically prayed that God would bring some kind of goodness out of what seemed to have the potential to blow up in all of their faces. She prayed for a miracle. She was just whispering "amen" when she heard the door to the library open. She reached for her eye mask, made sure it was secure, then turned around.

"Mr. Knightley, I presume," she said with her best attempt at a proper British accent, just the way she'd practiced it earlier this afternoon.

"Emma Woodhouse?" the guy said, playing along as he held his eye mask in place. As he came closer, his lips broke into a smile as if he was pleased to see her.

She peered closely at him. Was it possible? Was that Isaac? Had she really landed her dream date in this little game?

"You look very pretty, uh, Emma." With a plate of appetizers in his hand, he approached her.

She nodded. "Thank you. You look very nice too." She took in his dark gray pants, his old-fashioned light gray jacket which must've been rented from the drama department, and the narrow tie on the pale blue ruffled shirt. Okay, maybe he wasn't exactly eighteenth century, but he had certainly tried.

"So, we're supposed to get better acquainted," he said.

"Would you like to sit down?" She pointed to a pair of chairs flanking the window, and soon they were both seated and she didn't know what to say. She took a sip of punch and tried not to look too happy.

"I knew it was going to be you," he said quietly.

"Really?" She fingered the eye mask. "So you know who I am?"

"You're Emma."

"Yes, obviously. And you're Mr. Knightley."

He chuckled. "You really don't know who I am?"

She grinned. "Yes, Isaac, I knew the minute I saw you."

He removed his mask. "Well, I knew as soon as Bryn told me I was supposed to dress as Mr. Knightley so I could go out with Emma Woodhouse."

"But you never told anyone?" She removed her mask now, glad to be rid of it.

"Those were the rules." He beamed at her.

"Well, I must admit that I was relieved to see it was you."

"Who did you think you'd get?"

She shrugged. "I was preparing myself for the worst."

"So I'm not the worst?"

She laughed. "Hardly."

"Well, it was an interesting limo ride over here," he told her.

"What do you mean?"

"I mean, it was an interesting mix of guys."

She leaned toward him with curiosity. "Which guys?"

"Will I get in trouble if I tell you?"

She shrugged. "I don't see why. I mean, everyone knows who their dates are by now."

He slowly shook his head like he was in disbelief. "I'll just say this, there are some girls' faces I'd like to see right now. I'd like to know how they're reacting to their blind dates."

"What do you mean?" she said eagerly. "Tell me everything, Isaac!"

"Okay." He rubbed his chin thoughtfully. "Well, when the limo picked me up, only Kent was inside."

She nodded. "Yes. I picked Kent for Abby. I'm sure she'll be happy about that."

"Yeah. And he'll be happy too. The lucky guy."

Emma frowned. "Because he's with Abby?"

"Well, yeah, but not exactly. I meant because he got to wear pretty normal-looking clothes. I guess he's supposed to be from *The Hunger Games*. I can't remember his name."

"Peeta."

"Yeah, that's right. So anyway, Kent was already there. And next we picked up Darrell Zuckerman."

Emma blinked. "Seriously?"

"Uh-huh. I mean, I don't have anything against the guy. I know he's supposed to be some kind of genius. And everyone knows he's an atheist. But I honestly didn't expect to see him as one of the blind dates tonight. Kent and I were both pretty shocked. But we were friendly to him. He didn't seem to have any idea who he was going out with, but it seemed like he was being a good sport about it."

"What was he dressed as?" she asked eagerly.

"He had on a black suit. At first I teased him, asking him who died. Then he told me he was supposed to be from the Roaring Twenties. Some guy named Gatsby."

"Jay Gatsby," she explained. "He's Bryn's date."

Isaac looked stunned. "Bryn and Darrell? Wow, that's pretty random."

She slowly nodded. "Tell me about it. Cassidy set them up, and she's been totally freaking over it."

"She should be."

"Why?"

"Because Darrell told us that if his date went wrong, he

was going to take revenge on the girl who had set him up. He didn't say her name, but he did say he'd make her sorry."

"Poor Cass."

Isaac nodded grimly. "I can't imagine that Bryn will take this too well."

Emma felt slightly sick. "This could ruin the whole dance."

He frowned. "The whole dance? Does that mean we can't have fun?" He pointed to his clothes. "I mean, a guy dresses like this and you tell him that it's all for nothing?"

She forced a smile. "No, it's not for nothing. We'll have fun. But Cassidy probably won't. And Bryn . . . well, I hate to even think about that." She let out a sigh. "Who else was in the limo?"

"Okay, so the next guy who gets in is almost as weird as Darrell. Do you know Leonard Mansfield?"

"I know *who* he is." Emma grimaced. Poor Leonard was considered one of the geekiest guys at Northwood. "But I don't really know him."

"Well, you will after tonight."

"Oh." She pressed her lips together. Could this get any worse? She was almost afraid to ask. "So . . . uh . . . was Leonard dressed as, say, Romeo?"

Isaac nodded. "You nailed it, Emma. He said he got the costume from the drama department. He even had on tights, poor guy."

"Poor guy." She didn't even want to think of the fit Devon must be throwing right now. Perhaps it was a good thing they were all meeting in private after all. Cassidy had worked to convince Emma of this, causing her to be the swing vote that made certain it happened.

"Who's his date, anyway?"

"Devon."

"Devon?" Isaac looked properly shocked. "No way. Devon and Leonard? That's quite a match."

"Oh, yeah. She's dressed as Juliet. And I'm surprised we can't hear her screaming from here. But then she's in the parlor and that's on the other side of the house."

"I wonder who set Devon up with someone like Leonard."

Emma thought about this. "It has to be Abby." She shook her head. "That explains why she's been acting so weird lately."

"Huh?"

"Guilty conscience. Plus she's probably afraid that Devon is going to kill her. It's a good thing Abby is armed tonight."

Isaac laughed.

"Both Abby and Cassidy are in some serious hot water." Emma fingered a ribbon from her hat. "Speaking of Cassidy, I wonder who her date is tonight. Who was the last guy in the limo? That would have to be her date."

"A guy I never met before. He's really new to school. His name is Russell—I didn't catch the last name. The poor guy was having some severe allergy problems."

"Allergy problems?"

"Yeah, he was dressed as a scarecrow and I think the straw was making him sneeze."

"Oh, yeah. That makes sense."

"The sneezing?"

"No, that he's a scarecrow. Cassidy is Dorothy from *The Wizard of Oz*. Anyway, how did he seem?"

"Sneezy?"

Emma laughed. "Well, at least Cassidy ought to be civilized to him. I can't say the same for Bryn and Devon and their poor dates."

"Hopefully someone will get him some allergy medicine before the dance."

Emma smiled at Isaac. "I'm so glad you're my date," she told him.

He grinned back. "Me too. I think we're the ones who got lucky tonight."

She looked at the clock up on the bookshelf and knew that it was almost time to join the others. However, she really didn't want to. She wouldn't have minded remaining in here and talking to Isaac all night long. She definitely had gotten lucky with her blind date. Of course, this reminded her that she owed Bryn some serious gratitude for setting her up. And then she remembered how angry and jealous she'd gotten at Bryn for merely talking to Isaac a week or so ago. Emma had been such a witch about it. And sweet Bryn had probably just been working on this date for her.

Now Bryn was stuck with the likes of Darrell Zuckerman. Emma felt unreasonably disappointed at Cassidy. Could Cassidy have done any worse? To match poor Bryn with someone like Darrell Zuckerman—a geek and an atheist. It wasn't just unkind, it was downright mean. Emma glanced uneasily at Isaac as he finished off his punch. Bryn had landed the perfect date for Emma tonight. As a result, Emma owed Bryn big time. So even if Emma had to share Isaac with Bryn at the dance tonight, it was the least she could do. Somehow she had to make it up to Bryn. She just hoped that Isaac wouldn't mind. But then why would he mind? What normal teenage guy wouldn't love to go out on the dance floor with a girl as stunning as Bryn Jacobs?

As Abby went down the stairs to the basement, she pretended that she'd been banished to the dungeon. Really, it seemed fairly just. Okay, she knew that Bryn had sent her down here because she was the only one not wearing heels. Although come to think of it, Emma had on ballet flats. But maybe Abby deserved to be banished. And even if they locked the door and threw away the key, she wasn't sure she'd really care.

As she sat down in Mrs. Jacobs's favorite rocking chair, all Abby could think about was how angry Devon was going to be in a few minutes. Abby hated to think of what Devon would say or do when Leonard Mansfield, dressed in tights, walked into the parlor and declared himself to be Devon's Romeo. Abby was thankful this was a scene she would not have to witness. And maybe, if she got lucky, Abby's date would mysteriously disappear and Abby would be forgotten down here for the duration of the evening.

She extracted an arrow from her quiver and examined it

for straightness. She hadn't actually shot her bow for more than a year, but the idea of shooting something tonight felt extremely appealing. She stood up, then got out her bow and carefully set the arrow into place, aiming it at the far wall of shelves. Of course, she wouldn't actually shoot it—she didn't want to put a hole into anything down here—but it would feel good to shoot or throw or kick something.

"Katniss?"

Abby was so surprised that she nearly let go of the arrow. She hadn't even heard anyone on the stairs. She released the tension on the bowstring and lowered the bow, slowly turning around to see who was here. The voice was familiar, yet she wasn't quite sure who it was. Then seeing someone dressed similar to Peeta—except that he had a mask over his eyes—reminded her that she hadn't put on her own eye mask.

"Are you going to shoot me?" he asked as he approached her with a big grin on his face.

"No." She slipped the arrow back into the quiver and looked around for her eye mask. "I was just—uh—sorry, I forgot to put on my mask." She picked it up and sighed. "Although I suspect you would've guessed who I am." She went closer to him, peering curiously. "And I'm pretty sure I know who you are now."

His smile faded. "Really?"

"Kent?"

He nodded. "You're disappointed?"

"No, no." She put the bow back over her shoulder. "Not at all. Did I sound disappointed?"

"You look disappointed."

"I'm sorry." She forced a shy smile. "I'm not disappointed at all. I hope you're not disappointed."

"I hoped it was going to be you."

"Oh." She nodded. "Good."

"But you don't seem happy, Abby. What's up?"

She looked at the heavily loaded plate in his hand, realizing that she'd forgotten to bring down her own plate of food. "Can I have that?" She pointed to the crab cake on top.

"Sure."

She took it and slowly ate a few bites. "You're right," she admitted. "I'm feeling a little out of sorts tonight."

"Maybe it's the costume," he suggested. "Although you look great in it. But Katniss was a real warrior. Do you feel like fighting with someone?"

She laughed. "To be honest, I was feeling like hitting something right now."

"But not me?" he asked.

"No, not you. Definitely not you."

"So what's going on then?"

"These stupid blind dates," she said as she sat back down in the rocker.

"But I'm your blind date," he protested as he perched on the edge of a craft table and bit into a crab cake. "You're confusing me, Abby."

"Sorry. The truth is, I'm feeling pretty apprehensive about the blind date I set up for Devon."

"Oh? Which guy was Devon's date?" He chuckled. "I gotta admit there were some real characters in the limo tonight. And I'm not just talking about literary characters either, if you know what I mean."

"I know." She grimaced. "So did you meet Romeo by any chance?"

"You mean *Leonard Mansfield*?"

She nodded grimly.

"Leonard is Devon's date?" He burst into laughter.

"Devon is going to kill me."

Kent pointed to her bow. "But you're armed and dangerous, Katniss. You can take her."

She glared at him.

"Except you better be careful about what you eat or drink at the dance. Wasn't there poison involved with Romeo and Juliet's unfortunate demise?"

"Not helping." She hopped up and snatched a cheese puff from his plate, popping it into her mouth.

"If it's any consolation, old Leonard looked pretty good as Romeo. We didn't even know who he was at first."

"Really?"

"Yeah. With that dark curly hair he looks kind of Italian. Plus he's sporting a dark mustache. And with his eye mask on, I doubt anyone will guess who he is."

"You think so?" Suddenly Abby was feeling hopeful.

"It's possible."

"And we weren't supposed to take off our eye masks until we get to the dance," she said thoughtfully.

"So are you feeling better now?"

She gave him a relaxed smile. "As a matter of fact I am. Except that I'm hungry." She snatched his last crab cake.

"Hey, so am I."

"I was so worried about tonight that I barely ate any dinner," she told him. "And that was after a long, hard basketball practice too."

"I hear you girls are going to have a good team this year."

She nodded as she chewed. "How about you? Are you going to play this year?"

He shook his head. "Nah. I'm not that good."

"You used to be," she reminded him.

"I'm more into music these days," he told her.

"I'm more into food." She laughed as she grabbed up his last cheese puff. "Thanks!"

"I think this whole *Hunger Games* thing has gone straight to your head," he said jokingly.

"I know—why don't we sneak back upstairs and get some more food?" she suggested.

He nodded like a coconspirator. "I like how you think, Katniss."

"Come on, Peeta, I'll show you how it's done."

He laughed as they pretended to sneak up the stairs.

"Quiet," she warned. "We don't want any of the others to hear us."

"Yeah," he whispered. "More food for us, right?"

"That's right." She suppressed a giggle as she quietly opened the door and looked around. "Coast is clear," she told him.

They tiptoed out and Abby led him directly to the dining room where the food was still set up and no one was around. "Looks like we have the place to ourselves," she said as she reached for another crab cake.

"Should we bag up the food and make a run for it?" he teased.

"Nah. Let's just take our chances and eat it here." She set a crab cake on his plate. "My payback."

"Thanks." He grinned. "I'm sure glad you were my blind date, Abby. I had a feeling it would be you."

"How did you guess?"

"Who else would want to dress like Katniss?"

"Oh . . ." She nodded as she chewed.

"And you look pretty hot in that outfit too."

She laughed. "Bryn and Devon sure didn't think so."

He shrugged. "Shows what they know."

"By the way, who set you up for me?"

"Emma."

Abby knew that she owed Emma a big hug—at the very least.

"But Devon tried to get me."

"Really?"

"Yeah, we have fitness training together. She thought she could talk me into being someone else's blind date. But she ended up getting this new guy."

"What new guy?" she asked curiously.

"His name is Russell."

"And what was he dressed as?"

"A scarecrow. We dubbed him the Sneezing Scarecrow."

"Really?"

"Poor guy. I guess he's got allergies."

Abby laughed.

"Anyway, he seems pretty nice. And he really doesn't know anyone. So it was nice that he could do this. Well, except for the allergy thing. But I think Bryn's grandmother gave him something for it. Hopefully he'll be okay."

"Yeah. He's Cassidy's blind date, and I'm guessing she'll be nice to him." Abby frowned. "Unlike some girls."

"Still worried about Devon?"

"I wish I wasn't." Abby glanced down the hall that went to the parlor. She knew that was where Juliet was supposed to be meeting Romeo. "I don't hear any screaming and yelling going on," she said quietly.

"I'll bet Devon hasn't figured it out yet," he assured her as he refilled his punch cup.

"Let's cross our fingers that she doesn't figure it out . . . not until the dance." She held up crossed fingers. "And then I'll do the best I can to do damage control." She looked hopefully at Kent. "Maybe you can help."

"Help?"

"Like if Devon starts to throw a fit, maybe you could offer to dance with her. Kind of a distraction technique, you know?"

He nodded. "Sure. This really is similar to *The Hunger Games*—first we're stealing food and now we're strategizing together. I like it."

She grinned. "Hopefully no one will get killed."

"I'll be watching your back, Katniss."

"Thanks, Peeta."

"And you should know that dressing like Peeta has transformed me into my little sister's superhero. She made me promise to send her pictures of Katniss." He reached in his pocket to extract his phone. "You mind?"

"Not at all." She posed as he snapped some shots, even pulling out her bow and arrow and taking aim at Mrs. Jacobs's rooster-shaped cookie jar. Then he took some pictures of the two of them together. Suddenly, they could hear the others coming out.

"It's time," she said nervously. "Let the games begin."

He chuckled. "And don't forget—I'm on your team."

"Thanks. I'm holding you to it." She snatched a crab cake from his plate and laughed. "Better grab what you want before the others get here. I know Bryn plans to hurry us out to the dance." Come to think of it, Abby was now eager to get this show on the road too. The sooner they got to the dance the better. It would be easier to handle Devon's hissy fit in a crowded room with curious onlookers. And with Kent helping to distract Devon on the dance floor, well, maybe it wouldn't be as horrible as Abby had imagined.

As Cassidy waited nervously in the sunroom, she knew that no matter who her blind date was, she would not complain. Not after what she'd done to Bryn. Of all the girls, Cassidy deserved to get the worst date of the night. If her date turned out to be what Bryn might consider "decent," Cassidy fully intended to talk him into trading places with Darrell Zuckerman. Sure, it might seem odd for Daisy Buchanan to be dancing with a scarecrow, but if he was a good guy and if this switch pacified Bryn, Cassidy did not care.

Besides that, Cassidy told herself, Darrell Zuckerman was not that bad. Well, unless he was angry at you. That could be bad. She nervously stroked Toto's plush fur. "I think I know how Dorothy felt," she whispered, "when she was waiting for the Wicked Witch of the West to destroy her."

"Dorothy?"

Cassidy looked up from where she was sitting in a wicker

chair to see a lanky-looking scarecrow leaning against the doorframe. Despite her previously gloomy thoughts, she couldn't help but smile as she stood to greet him. Feeling her eye mask to make sure it was in place, she went over and extended her hand. "And you must be my scarecrow."

He made a deep, loose-jointed bow, very similar to how the scarecrow in the movie would do it. "At your service, Dorothy." He reached out and patted the stuffed dog. "And Toto too."

For what seemed like the first time in days, she laughed. "Want to sit down?"

"Y—ye—yes!" He let out a big sneeze.

"Bless you."

"Thanks. And sorry. My allergies kicked up tonight." He sniffled as he stuffed a loose piece of straw back into the front of his red plaid shirt. "This isn't helping much."

"Oh, dear." She frowned. "Want to take the straw out before we go to—"

"No!" He clutched his chest protectively. "Where would I be without my straw filling? Just a pile of old clothes? I think not, dear Dorothy."

She laughed again. This guy was good.

"Besides, the kind lady of the house—I believe her name is Mrs. Jacobs—generously gave me a Benadryl pill." He sneezed again as he sat down. "Hopefully it won't make me sleepy. She promised to brew me a cup of coffee before we leave just in case." Now he seemed to really study Cassidy. "You make a very nice Dorothy," he said. It sounded like a sincere compliment.

"And you're a great Scarecrow too." She tilted her head to one side. "But you don't seem familiar. Have we met before?"

"I honestly don't know," he confessed. "I don't recall meeting you." He smiled. "And I'm sure I would remember you." He reached over and gently tweaked a braid.

"Well, we're supposed to wear our eye masks until we get to the dance," she explained. "Although I'll bet most everyone has guessed who their date is by now."

"It'd be pretty hard for me to guess." He rubbed his nose as if he expected to sneeze again. "I'm new to Northwood. I don't really know anyone. Well, except for a few people in my classes. And the guys in the limo tonight. And, of course, the girl who asked me to do this."

"Which girl was that?" she asked curiously.

"Devon Fremont."

"Really?" Cassidy was surprised. Devon could've done far worse. In fact, Cassidy had done far, far worse for Bryn, but she was trying not to think about that right now.

"Yeah, Devon's in my fitness-training class. She was trying to get Kent for your blind date, but he already had plans. As a matter of fact, he's here tonight."

"What's he dressed as?"

"That guy from *The Hunger Games*."

She nodded. "That would be Abby's date."

He shook his head. "How do you keep it all straight?"

"I'm actually just putting it all together myself."

He pointed to his head. "Maybe I would too—if I only had a brain."

She laughed again. "You're pretty funny. But do you have a name or do I call you Scarecrow?"

"Scarecrow is fine for now," he told her. "Maybe after I meet the wizard and get a brain . . . maybe I'll come up with a name by then."

"So how long have you been at Northwood?" she asked.

"Not even two weeks."

"That must be hard . . . being new, I mean." She frowned. "Although, under the right circumstances, it could be nice to get a fresh new start. That actually sounds pretty good to me right now."

"Why?"

She let out a sigh. "It's a long story."

"I think we still have about ten minutes."

And so, similar to how she'd spilled the beans to Emma, she told him about her stupid mistake of setting up the beautiful Bryn with someone like Darrell Zuckerman.

"You mean Jay Gatsby?"

"Yeah. That's him."

"He seemed like a nice guy to me."

She rolled her eyes. "Well, sure he's nice to you. He doesn't even know you. And as long as you don't cross him, he's fine. But I have seriously crossed him. He'll be enraged at me."

"For setting him up with a beautiful girl? Why would he be mad at you?"

"Because I *know* Bryn. She will not take this lying down. Neither will Darrell." She glanced at the door that led out to the garden. "In fact, it's taking all my self-control not to make a run for it right now."

"What if you're wrong?"

"I am wrong. I was wrong." Cassidy stood up now, pacing across the sunroom. "I don't know what got into me. Bryn could've had a date with any guy. I so did not have to pick Darrell Zuckerman."

"You said Bryn was your friend, right?"

Cassidy shrugged. "I guess."

"Friends forgive each other, don't they?"

"Yeah, maybe. I mean, Bryn might forgive me . . . eventually. But Darrell Zuckerman—it's no secret that he's an atheist, and since he promised to make my life miserable if I messed this up, well, I don't think he'll give me any grace on this."

Scarecrow slowly nodded. "That's rough, Dorothy." He pointed at her shoes. "Maybe you should click your heels together and get out of here."

She looked down at the glitter-coated red shoes and smiled. "I wish I could."

"But then I wouldn't get to take you to the dance," he said sadly.

"I'm sorry," she told him. "I didn't want to spoil your evening too. I'll stick around." She removed her eye mask. "But I guess we don't even need these masks right now. It's not like we'll recognize each other anyway."

He smiled as he removed his own. "You really make a pretty Dorothy."

"Thanks. You're a great Scarecrow too. I wish I was in better spirits."

He rubbed his chin as if he was thinking. "If I only had a brain, I would try to think of a way to help you out of this mess."

Despite her gloominess, she smiled.

"When I'm in bad straits, I sometimes ask myself a question," he said.

"What question?" she asked.

"What's the worst thing that could happen? You already said that you think your friend will forgive you . . . in time. But really, what is the worst thing this Jay Gatsby—or Darrell Zuckerman—can do to you? It's not like he's going to hire a hit man to take you out, is he?"

"No, probably not."

"So what would he do then?"

"Well, Darrell is super smart. Genius. And he's always struck me as a guy who doesn't play by the rules."

"Uh-huh? So what would he do?"

She thought hard. "The first thing I thought he might do is get me into some kind of trouble at school—you know, do something really clever and pin it on me—so that I'd get caught and possibly lose the college scholarships I've been working so hard toward."

"But how could you get caught—as you say—if you are innocent?"

"Like I said, Darrell is really smart . . . and devious. And the way he was talking to me—the threats he made—I have no doubt he would carry them out. He would get even."

"But it seems like even if he tried to do that, you would be innocent and your friends would know it. You could gather evidence and prove your innocence. And even if it was inconvenient, you could prove that he was the one to set you up and he'd be the one to get in trouble. You would be cleared."

"Do you want to be my lawyer? To help clear my name? If and when this happens?"

"Sure. I'd be happy to help you, Dorothy." He tapped his head. "If I only had a brain."

She laughed.

"See, that's the Dorothy I know. Brave and smart and determined. That's the girl who will get me to the wizard."

She pointed at the wall clock. "And get you to the dance."

He stood and made another low bow. "I am at your disposal."

"Then I guess this is it. We're off to see the wizard." She

linked her arm in his. "Or else we'll be carried away by the evil monkeys."

He reached up and touched his nose. "Hey, I'm not sneezing anymore."

"That's right."

"I take that as a good sign." He grinned as he replaced his eye mask. "This is going to be a good evening—for both of us."

"And Toto too." She patted the stuffed dog's head, forcing what she hoped looked like a brave smile. If Dorothy could be brave against all the foes that she had to face, why couldn't Cassidy be brave enough to face Bryn and Darrell? Scarecrow was right. By imagining the worst that could happen, she realized that she really had been blowing it out of proportion. Sure, she owed both Bryn and Darrell full apologies. But she would deliver them, and if those two refused to forgive and forget—well, she would just deal with it.

Devon hadn't told any of her friends that her mom had gone off with Rodney again. It wasn't Vegas, but it might as well have been since she was not coming back until Monday evening. And this time she had not even made any provision for Devon to camp out at Emma's house. Not that Devon wanted to. That hadn't gone so well the last time. Not only had Devon and Emma squabbled, but Emma's mom had seemed put out at Devon's mom for dumping Devon on her. And for that reason, Devon didn't plan to confide to any of her friends about her AWOL mom. She didn't even tell her aunt when she got her hair done. Devon figured if Mom hadn't bothered to tell anyone besides Devon, she must've wanted it to be a secret. And keeping it secret was exactly what Devon intended to do.

She also intended to make the most of her mom's absence. And to that end she had a plan. Of sorts. Okay, the plan was sketchy at best, but if all went well it could prove to be fun.

For starters, Devon had spent more than an hour cleaning house. Normally, housework was the last thing on Devon's mind, but since her mom was away for a few days, Devon decided it was time to do some "entertaining." And having laundry baskets and junk strewn all over the place was not exactly conducive to that. After the house was straightened up some, Devon did some exploring in her mom's bedroom, and just as she suspected, Mom had a secret stash of alcohol there. How convenient.

Devon had arranged the various bottles on the breakfast bar, along with some cans of soda, some glasses, a big bowl of Doritos, and a smaller bowl of peanuts. Okay, it wasn't The Ritz, but it would do. And since she was into living dangerously, Devon even made herself a drink, mixing vodka and Coke. Okay, maybe it wasn't a real drink with a fancy name, but it was definitely alcohol. And as soon as she had her Juliet costume on, and before Cassidy showed up to give her a ride over to Bryn's grandparents' house, Devon had chugged it down.

But Devon hadn't stopped there. She had also found a nice little flask in her mom's things. This she filled with straight vodka and tucked into the little embroidered purse that she was using with her Juliet costume. She had no idea what she really planned to do with the alcohol—well, besides have fun. And she intended to have fun!

Now Devon played with the strings of her purse as she sat in Mrs. Jacobs's front parlor. This old-fashioned room was filled with flowery-looking furnishings and carved antique pieces—almost like going back in time. As she waited, Devon was enjoying a happy little buzz and imagining her handsome Romeo taking her into his arms, telling her how beautiful she looked, and kissing her passionately.

She envisioned her Romeo as a hot guy like Lane Granger, Marcus Zimmerman, Kent Renner, or even Jason Levine—despite her claim that she was never speaking to that particular jerk again. She reached up to touch her curls, making sure they were still in place. Then she looked down at the wide, scooped neckline of the Juliet dress, ensuring that the low cut was making the most of her endowments. Where was Romeo anyway?

As if on cue, she heard the doorknob to the parlor turning, and there, dressed in all his glory—tights and poufy shorts and fluffy sleeves and all—stood her Romeo. And he didn't look half bad. Although the fake mustache would have to go. Romeo wasn't supposed to have a mustache! He was only a young teen. Okay, he was a hormone-driven young teen, but Devon felt certain he would not have a mustache.

"Juliet?" he said tentatively.

"Romeo, Romeo," she said dramatically. "Where hast thou been?"

"I—uh—I was in the limo."

"Yeah, I know." She rolled her eyes as she went closer to inspect her prize. Between the eye mask and mustache, it was impossible to guess. But he had good height. And his dark curly hair actually added to the whole Romeo look. She knew that Lane Granger had dark curly hair. And Kent had dark hair too. "You look familiar," she said as she checked him out carefully.

"You look familiar too, uh, Juliet." His voice cracked ever so slightly.

Naturally, she found that irritating. "Why don't we sit down," she said, returning to the flowered sofa and patting the spot next to her. "I see you got yourself something to eat."

"Uh-huh." He sat down a couple of feet from her, almost as if he was scared. Or intimidated. Well, that was okay. She knew that her looks sometimes intimidated guys, and she liked that.

"How was the limo ride?" she asked somewhat absently. She wanted to get him to talk, hoping she'd recognize his voice and figure out who he really was.

"Uh, it was okay."

"Anyone I know in the limo?" she asked.

"Just a scarecrow and the Gatsby guy and someone from *The Hunger Games.* And I can't remember who the other guy was supposed to be. A knight, I think."

"A knight?" Devon was confused. "Oh, you must mean Mr. Knightley."

"Yeah. That's it."

She adjusted her eye mask to see him better, hoping she could place him. "Really, Romeo," she said with irritation. "When did you grow the mustache?"

He laughed, reaching up to finger it. "Oh, that. It's not real."

"No!" She rolled her eyes dramatically. "I never would've guessed."

"You look really pretty," he said nervously and his voice broke again.

"Do you actually go to our school?" she demanded. "To Northwood?"

"Yeah, sure. Of course."

She pursed her lips. "Do I know you?"

"Of course. I'm Romeo, remember?"

"Oh, that's right." She folded her arms in front of her and crossed her legs. Something about this felt wrong. Really wrong.

"So, Romeo," she said in what she hoped was an enticing tone. "Tell me, who arranged this date? Which of my friends picked you out for me?" For some reason she suspected it was Bryn. It wouldn't surprise her if Bryn tried something like this—a way to humiliate Devon for taking the Juliet dress.

"Am I supposed to tell?" he asked.

"It doesn't matter now," she assured him. "We'll all find out tonight anyway."

"Oh, okay. Well, it was Abby."

"Abby?" Devon was surprised by this. Abby was usually a pretty thoughtful sort of girl. "So, tell me, Romeo . . . are you good friends with Abby?"

He shrugged. "Yeah. I guess so."

"Uh-huh . . . I see. . . ." Now she wondered if he was an athletic friend of Abby's. He didn't seem very muscular, but perhaps he played soccer or lacrosse. And those kids usually had brains. And sometimes their families had money. And if that was the case, maybe Devon should just make the best of it with him. After all, if this kid was athletic and had both brains and money—how bad could it be? And he didn't even seem terribly bad looking with all that dark curly hair. It might even be fun to do some serious flirting with a guy like this. However, something about her date did not quite add up. Nothing in the way he spoke or acted seemed to suggest he was particularly intelligent. And he lacked confidence, which she found irritating.

"Would you mind excusing me?" he asked suddenly.

"Excusing you? For what?"

"I—uh—I need to use the, uh, the restroom."

Devon rolled her eyes, then waved him away. "Yes, please—go and take care of . . . *whatever*."

After he left, Devon suspected that it was nearly time for them to all reconvene. And since she couldn't wait to get her hands—or even her claws—onto Abby, she decided to venture out. As luck would have it, she discovered Abby and Kent in the dining room. And the two of them seemed intent upon making pigs of themselves.

"Did you save anything for the rest of us?" As Devon reached for a carrot stick, she carefully eyed Abby, trying to decide how to handle this.

"Hey, we are part of *The Hunger Games*," Kent told her. "We hold food in very high esteem."

Abby giggled nervously. "How's your date?"

"What date?" Devon locked her eyes onto Abby. Was it her imagination, or was Abby actually squirming?

"Your blind date," Abby said.

"I don't know, Abby. How *is* my date?"

Abby turned to Kent as if looking for help.

"Where is your date?" Kent asked Devon.

"He went to the little boys' room," Devon said evenly, keeping her eyes locked on Abby.

"That's a good idea." Abby stepped back from Devon. "Maybe I'll make a visit to the little girls' room myself."

"Not without me, you won't." Devon glared at her.

"I'll warn you," Abby told her. "It's a one-seater."

Kent laughed as some of the others started to trickle into the dining room, including Bryn's grandparents, who were armed with cameras.

"Excuse me," Abby quietly told Kent. "I'll be right back." And before Devon could intervene—and as the room grew crowded and busy and loud—Abby exited the dining room and disappeared out of sight.

"Let me through here," Devon insisted as she attempted to push past Emma and Isaac and Bryn's grandfather. But even as she got beyond them, Kent managed to block the door by doing a silly little dance as he pretended to be unable to decide which side to go to. Naturally this slowed her down considerably.

When she finally got out of the room, she had no idea which way Abby had gone, but she was madder than ever now. Since she was Bryn's best friend, Abby probably knew her way around this big house much better than Devon. Even so, Devon was determined to find Abby and have a word with her—and to find out exactly who was playing Romeo.

Devon checked the laundry room and the powder room and even the big four-car garage. She opened the basement door, peering down the dark stairs. Then she went upstairs, and after checking behind several doors with no success, she heard Bryn downstairs calling out.

"Okay, everyone, it's time to go to the dance. Everyone into the limo now. Let's go, people! Where is Devon?"

"I'm coming," Devon yelled as she hurried down the stairs. As she reached the foyer, she could see that the others were already on their way out to the limo. Since it was raining, everyone was making a dash to the car, laughing as they went. Having fun.

"It's about time," Bryn said when she saw Devon. Then she grabbed the hand of a guy dressed like Jay Gatsby. "Come on, let's go."

"There you are." Romeo nervously rubbed his hands together as he looked at Devon. "Everything, uh, okay?"

"Oh, yeah." She narrowed her eyes. "Everything is just peachy."

"Ready to go then?"

"I am *more* than ready," she snapped. Then she looped her arm into his and literally dragged him toward the door. "Are you coming or not?"

"I need to get my coat." He slowed down to reach for a beige jacket hanging by the door. "Don't you have a coat, uh, Juliet?"

"I don't need a coat," she growled. "I've got your love to keep me warm, *right*?"

"Uh, yeah, I guess so."

"Come on!" She gave his arm a sharp tug. "Let's go."

They were the last ones into the limo, and the others—all who seemed to be in surprisingly good spirits—teased them as they got inside.

"Figures Romeo and Juliet were dillydallying," Emma said.

"You know how star-crossed lovers can be," Bryn added.

Devon searched the limo for Abby and Kent. "I want to sit there," she demanded, pointing to where Emma was sitting.

"Sorry, that seat's taken," Isaac told her.

"Then that side," Devon pointed to where Bryn and her date were seated.

"Sorry," Bryn said. "We're good to go," she called out to the driver, knocking on the window between them.

"There's room here," Cassidy said as the limo took off. But Cassidy and her scarecrow friend were clear on the other end.

"We better sit," Romeo said as he went over to sit by the scarecrow. "How's the allergy going?" he asked.

"Better. The medicine helped."

Devon glared at Abby, who was ignoring her, as she sat down next to Cassidy. "This sucks!" she grumbled.

"What's wrong?" Cassidy asked with what seemed genuine concern.

"My date," Devon whispered. "Abby set me up with a geek."

Cassidy leaned over to peer at Romeo. She shrugged. "Seems okay to me," she whispered back. "Makes a good-looking Romeo, don't you think?"

"I think he's a dud," Devon hissed.

"Give him a chance," Cassidy urged.

"Why?" Devon glared at her.

"Why not?"

Devon folded her arms tightly across her front, staring straight forward to where Abby was sitting with Bryn and Emma and their dates—watching how they were all laughing and joking and thoroughly enjoying themselves. Well, except for Abby. She was the quiet one of the group. Oh, she tried to act like she was engaging, but she clearly was not. Abby obviously felt guilty. She should feel guilty.

Devon looked back at Cassidy now, suddenly remembering that she'd set Cass up with a somewhat nerdy guy. "Uh, how's your blind date?" Devon asked her quietly.

"Great." Cassidy turned to grin at her date. "He's a fine Scarecrow."

"Oh, well . . . good. Glad to hear it."

Cassidy gave Devon a knowing look. "Don't you mean that you're *surprised* to hear it?"

Devon shrugged. "It's a blind date. Who knows how it will go?"

"That's right," Cassidy told her. "Same way for you, right?"

Devon looked over to where Romeo was sitting next to the scarecrow and looking very uneasy. With his crooked fake mustache, and wearing his beige coat over his costume with his long, skinny legs clad in black tights and sticking out, he looked like a total goofball. She looked down at her own dress. She knew she looked great in it. She knew that most guys would be glad to be her date. And yet she got stuck with *that*.

She looked back at Abby again, and this time she caught Abby looking at her. They locked eyes, and Devon glared at her so-called friend.

"Hey, Devon," Bryn said lightly. "What's troubling you?"

Devon narrowed her eyes. "What makes you think I'm troubled about something?"

"You look like you want to murder someone," Bryn said.

"The only person that Juliet kills is herself," Emma said sadly. "Hopefully you're not taking your role too seriously."

"Thanks for caring," Devon snarled at her.

Emma got up now, coming over to sit between Cassidy and Devon. "Come on, Devon," she said gently. "We all know you're ticked. But why not make the best of it? You're with friends. Just have fun."

"Have fun?" Devon glanced over at her geeky Romeo and tried not to gag. "Seriously?" she hissed. "With that?"

"Give him a chance," Emma said quietly. "He seems nice to me."

"To *you*." Devon rolled her eyes. "You and I are different. Or haven't you noticed?"

"This is only one evening," Emma reminded her. "And we've all agreed to share our dates with you. Isaac is more than willing to dance with you. Abby told me that Kent is too."

Devon folded her arms even more tightly in front of her. *Great*—her friends were offering her their castoffs now. Like she was some kind of lame charity case. Like they felt sorry for her. Well, nobody needed to feel sorry for Devon Fremont.

And if they thought she was going to act all grateful and sweet while they allowed their dates a dance or two with her, they had better think again. Devon was out for revenge tonight. She wasn't exactly sure how she would get it. But she was determined she would. She wasn't dressed like this for nothing. If a girl couldn't turn on the charm and turn a few male heads in a gown like this, well, then she might as well just go home!

I've never seen Devon this mad," Emma told Bryn as they went into the restroom together to fix a wardrobe malfunction on Bryn's dress. Some of the beads had gotten caught together, causing the dress to bunch and hike up in an unbecoming way in the back. Emma had kindly offered to help straighten it out.

"I know," Bryn said quietly. "When the masks came off and Devon saw that it was Leonard Mansfield, I thought she was going to slug him."

"Poor Leonard."

"At least the rest of us are trying to make him feel better." Bryn took advantage of her spot by the mirror to touch up her lipstick. "I've danced with him twice already."

"Me too."

"I told Abby to watch her back while we were gone," Bryn said as she slipped the lipstick back into her little beaded bag.

"Cassidy promised to keep an eye on the situation."

"Kent seems to be staying close to Abby," Bryn said with pride. "I'm so glad I got him for Abby's date."

"Yeah, except that's probably making it even harder on Devon. The more she sees the rest of us having a good time the madder she gets."

"And flirtier too." If anyone had told Bryn that she could possibly be upset by a girl flirting with Darrell Zuckerman, she never would've believed it. And yet when Bryn caught Devon attempting to charm her Great Gatsby, she had felt seriously jealous. Of course, she had not shown it.

"Tell me about it," Emma muttered as she worked on the beads. "Even after I told Devon I'd gladly share Isaac with her, she's still going after him like she wants to—wants to—well, *you know*."

"Just be glad that Isaac isn't taking the bait."

"Not yet he's not." Emma sounded worried.

"And he won't," Bryn proclaimed. "Isaac is into you, Emma. Can't you see that?"

"What I see is Devon—make that *Juliet*—foisting her ample cleavage right into Isaac's face." Emma made a growling sound. "Seriously, how is a prim Jane Austen character supposed to compete with that hussy?"

"And to think Devon is your best friend," Bryn said sadly. "Anyway, she used to be."

"Devon still has a lot to learn about being a friend—to anyone. Including herself."

Bryn leaned her head around in an attempt to see how Emma was doing. "Isn't it fixed yet?"

"It's almost there."

"Hurry," Bryn urged. "No telling what Devon is doing to our guys while we're gone."

"Yeah, while the mice are away—"

"That cat will be a big fat rat," Bryn finished.

"There," Emma declared as she stood. "I got it. Hopefully it won't snag up like that anymore now."

"Thanks." Bryn leaned in to the mirror, adjusting her glittery hair band and smoothing her hair into place. "We better get back to do damage control."

"It's so aggravating," Emma said as they left. "If Devon would just straighten up, we could all be having such a great time tonight."

"I guess it's true what they say—misery really does love company."

Emma turned and looked into Bryn's eyes. "Let's not let her win, Bryn."

"What do you mean?"

"I mean let's cut her off. We're all trying so hard to help her, letting her dance with our dates. Dancing with her date. Why don't we just set her adrift and let her fend for herself?"

"Really?" Bryn was surprised. Emma was usually the soft heart of the bunch. Especially when it came to Devon. "You're okay with that?"

"Tonight I am. It's like Devon has made her choice to play the spoiled brat. If we play along we're only encouraging her."

"Enabling her," Bryn added.

"Yeah. Just say *no* to enabling," Emma proclaimed as they went back into the dance.

"Okay. You tell Cass and I'll tell Abby. From this point on we are all cutting Juliet off. If she doesn't want to dance with Romeo, she can just sit and watch the rest of us. Agreed?"

Emma nodded. "Agreed."

Bryn actually liked this plan, but when she whispered it

to Abby, she could tell that Abby was worried. "You think Devon is going to take it lying down?"

"I don't really care. I don't even care if Devon throws herself on the ground and kicks and screams. If she wants to keep acting like a spoiled brat, making a fool of herself, let her. Not only that, but I think Devon should be kicked out of the DG. She has broken at least three or four rules tonight."

Abby's dark eyes grew wide, but then Kent came up from behind, handing her a drink. "I'll explain it to him," Abby said quietly.

Bryn nodded. Now she went over to tell Darrell the new game plan.

"I like it," he told her.

"Really?" She reached over to wipe a cookie crumb from his chin. "And I thought maybe you were getting into Juliet. I mean, she is a good dancer."

He grinned. "She's not my type, *Daisy*. You should know that."

Bryn laughed. "Yes, of course, Jay. I nearly forgot how devoted Jay is to Daisy."

"Ready to go shake a leg again?"

"You bet!"

As Bryn and Darrell went to the dance floor, she noticed that Emma and Isaac were already out there. And then Cass and her scarecrow came out, followed by Abby and Kent. Bryn glanced over to the table the five couples had been sharing and couldn't help but feel a little satisfaction to see that Juliet was sitting across the table from Romeo with a very dour expression. *Good*, Bryn thought. *Let Little Miss Snooty Pants stew for a while*. Maybe she'd come to her senses. And if she didn't—well, maybe the DG really should send her packing.

The four couples danced a few more dances before Bryn was ready to take another break, but when she and Darrell returned to their table, Devon was gone. "Where's Juliet?" Bryn asked Leonard.

He shrugged. "I don't know. She took off several dances ago."

The others were coming to the table now and the girls, feeling sorry for Leonard, took turns with him on the dance floor. But Devon was nowhere to be seen.

"Have you seen Devon anywhere?" Bryn said to Abby as the two of them went to get something from the snack table.

Abby shook her head as she reached for a brownie. "No."

"I wonder where she went." Bryn glanced around the crowded room.

"Home?" Abby ventured.

"The dance will be over pretty soon." Bryn took a sip of punch. "Do you think Devon will show up when the limo gets here? Should we wait for her?"

"I have no idea."

"The limo service might charge us extra if we try to get them to wait," Bryn pointed out.

"I think if Devon's not out there, we should just go. I'm guessing she went home. She was pretty mad. I haven't seen her on the dance floor at all." Abby scanned across the room. "And trust me, I've been watching for her."

"Afraid she's going to stab you in the back?"

Abby made a nervous laugh. "Well, I'm pretty sure she thinks I stabbed her in the back."

"Devon shouldn't throw stones," Bryn pointed out. "I mean, she set Cass up with a guy that she clearly thought was a loser. She even admitted that to me—she couldn't believe that Cassidy wasn't ticked."

"Russell is really nice," Abby said, "and he makes a great Scarecrow."

"Cass likes him well enough." Bryn took another sip. "Maybe not as a boyfriend, but she said that he's fun."

"Too bad Devon couldn't have taken a lesson from her. Or from you," Abby said, pointing at Bryn.

"You mean because of Darrell?"

Abby nodded as she chewed the last of her brownie.

"The truth is I almost did the same thing as Devon." Bryn held her thumb and forefinger close together. "I came this close to sending the poor boy home."

"Really?" Abby looked shocked.

"Yeah. I'm embarrassed to admit it. Poor Darrell, I didn't even give him a chance at first."

"What made you change your mind?"

"Something Gram had said to me earlier." Bryn thought back to that moment. "In fact, she said the exact same thing to Devon."

"Apparently Devon wasn't listening."

"I guess not." Bryn saw the guys waving at them. "I think it's the last dance." She tossed her punch cup into the trash. "Let's go!"

Poor Romeo had to sit by himself as the other four couples headed back for the last dance. Bryn felt sorry for him, but midway through the dance, Abby and Kent returned to the table to sit with him. Bryn suspected this was because Abby was still feeling guilty for setting him up. However, Leonard seemed like a pretty good sport. He probably wouldn't hold it against her. If he wanted to be angry at anyone, he should target Devon. She was the one who messed up tonight.

After the dance ended, they went back to their table and

collected their stuff. Everyone seemed to be in good spirits. Well, everyone but Leonard.

"The limo should be here by now," Bryn told them.

"Is Devon going home with us?" Leonard asked.

"No one has seen her," Abby told him.

"I texted her," Emma said, "but she's giving me the silent treatment."

"I think she already went home," Cassidy told Leonard.

"Oh . . . okay." Leonard looked slightly relieved.

Before long, they were all loaded into the limo. Everyone except Devon, that is. As the limo pulled away, it got very quiet.

"I hope you don't blame yourself for Devon's bad manners," Bryn told Leonard.

"Oh, well . . . uh, I guess not."

"Good," Cassidy said. "Because you were great as Romeo, and there's no excuse for how badly Devon treated you."

"Yeah," Abby chimed in. "I hope you didn't have too bad a time, Leonard."

His face broke into a smile. "I actually kinda had fun. I mean, uh, it wasn't *all* fun. But some of it was fun. And you guys were nice to, uh, dance with me like you did."

"I'm sorry Devon wasn't nicer to you," Emma told him.

"Well, uh, maybe if she hadn't been drinking," he said quietly.

"Drinking?" Emma's blue eyes grew wide. "What do you mean?"

"I mean, well, some people get mean when they drink. You know?" Leonard frowned. "I have an uncle like that."

"Are you saying that you think Devon was drinking?" Bryn asked him. "I mean, drinking alcohol?"

He nodded, swallowing so hard that his Adam's apple bobbed up and down. "Uh-huh."

"Are you certain about that?" Emma demanded. "I mean, how do you know?"

"She, uh, she had this flask in her purse." Leonard looked uneasy, like he'd said too much. "I guess I thought you guys, uh, that you knew about it. I wasn't trying to rat her out."

"Seriously?" Abby leaned forward. "You saw Devon drinking alcohol? How do you know it was alcohol?"

"I asked her what it was."

"And what did she say?" Kent pressed.

"Vodka." Leonard grimly shook his head. "I've never touched the stuff, but I think it's pretty strong."

"Devon drinks vodka?" Bryn turned to Emma. "Did you know about this?"

Emma slowly shook her head with a stunned expression. "I've known Devon my whole life. I realize she experimented with alcohol a little—at her other school. But she told me she didn't like it. And I was pretty sure she didn't do it anymore. Not since transferring to Northwood, anyway. I can't believe she'd drink at a school dance. What if she'd been caught?"

"Have you ever *seen* her drinking?" Cassidy asked Emma.

"Never."

"Well, I saw her," Leonard declared as if giving testimony in a court of law.

"Are you going to tell on her?" Bryn asked him. "I mean, you could get her into some pretty serious trouble at school."

He looked uncertain. "Well, no, uh, I don't see why I'd do that."

"Yeah, man, don't go and do that," Kent warned him. "It would make us all look bad. We'd all get called in."

"He's right," Darrell agreed. "And it's not that I have a

problem having a beer now and then. But not at a school dance." He chuckled. "Well, unless you want to get kicked out of this school."

"Do you still want to get kicked out of this school?" Cassidy asked him.

He shrugged, giving them all a half smile. "Not so much now."

Bryn gently elbowed him. "Yeah, it helps when you have friends, huh?"

He nodded.

"I realize I don't know you guys too well," Russell said quietly. "But I had a good time tonight. And even though Devon messed up, I'm glad she asked me to be Cassidy's blind date." He turned to Cass. "I had fun. Thanks."

The group got more lively now, remembering fun moments from the dance and retelling how worried they'd felt about their blind dates earlier in the evening. When it was time to drop the girls off, Bryn felt sad to see this part of the evening come to an end.

"The girls all get out here," she announced.

"Not the guys too?" Darrell teased.

"Well, I suppose you can get out if you want," she teased back. "But you can't come inside with us. Not unless you want my dad to meet you at the door with his shotgun."

"No thanks." Darrell held up his hands. "But is it okay if we walk you to the front door?"

"Why, Jay Gatsby, I would be personally disappointed if you didn't," she said in her best Daisy imitation.

Everyone except Leonard got out at Bryn's house, and she put her forefinger to her lips, reminding them to keep it down since her parents had probably gone to bed by now.

"So this is where the lovely Daisy Buchanan lives," Darrell said quietly as he walked her up to the porch.

"Yes, well, this little cottage is not quite as elegant as my mansion on the water," she said with her southern accent. "But it will do in a pinch."

He chuckled. "I had fun tonight, Bryn. Thanks for being such a good sport."

"Good sport?" She frowned. "Don't you think I had fun too?"

"I was hoping you did." He looked uncomfortable now.

"Well, I most certainly did." She held out her hand to him and said with the accent, "And since this was our first date, I will offer you my hand, Mr. Gatsby."

He grinned as he took it, giving it a firm shake.

"And I will look forward to getting better acquainted with you in the future," she said in a proper tone, trying to imitate Daisy.

"As will I." He released her hand, made a slight bow, and returned to the limo.

Bryn knew that the others were saying goodnight too, and not wanting to ruin anyone's special moment, she quietly unlocked the door and went inside to wait. It wasn't long until Cassidy joined her.

"Are Emma and Abby coming?" Bryn removed her shoes. "I want to get out of this dress and relax."

"They're still out there with their beaus," Cassidy whispered.

"K-i-s-s-i-n-g?" Bryn said in a teasing tone.

"Maybe." Cassidy giggled. "I wasn't looking."

"We'll get their story later," Bryn whispered.

Emma and Abby eventually came into the house, both of them giggling.

"Shhh," Bryn warned. "I promised we'd keep it quiet until we got downstairs."

Now she ushered her three friends through the semi-dark house and down the stairs. "Okay," she announced. "It's safe."

"Wow, look at this food," Cassidy declared as she stopped at the kitchenette counter that was loaded with snacks. She plucked up a brownie. "Those bunko ladies know how to eat."

"And that's only part of it." Bryn pointed at the fridge. "Mom said she'd put the perishable foods in there. But I'm getting out of this dress first."

Everyone agreed that they should get into something more comfortable, but before long they were all pigging out on the bunko leftovers. For the most part, Bryn decided, it had been a great night. Well, sure, there had been a few little bumps along the way, but all in all, Bryn felt the evening had been a success. Except for Devon. Bryn wasn't even sure what to think about that. On one hand, she felt a tiny bit sorry for Devon. But on the other hand, Devon probably deserved whatever it was she had gotten—or was going to get.

The last thing Emma wanted to think about tonight was Devon Fremont. And yet she could hardly think of anything else. As the four girls lounged in Bryn's cozy basement, wearing sweats and pajamas and picking at the yummy bunko leftovers, Emma was painfully aware that one member of the DG was MIA.

Emma had discreetly checked her phone a couple of times since they got back. She figured that Devon would text her before the night was over, but so far there was nothing—not a word. As much as part of Emma wanted to totally ignore her spoiled friend, she went ahead and sent Devon a short text asking how she was doing.

Emma knew Devon well enough to know that even if she was seriously ticked, she would still text. In fact, some of Devon's longest messages were the result of extreme angst. Either that or she would simply send a blunt demand that Emma call her ASAP, because Devon was a talker. She always needed to talk through her troubles, and Emma was always her best listener. But so far Devon appeared to be giving Emma the silent treatment tonight.

"Okay, it's your turn," Bryn said, pointing to Emma. "Time to rate your date."

Bryn had led off in the *rate your date* portion of their evening. She confessed how she'd nearly made the same mistake Devon had made and blown Darrell off earlier in the evening but how she had controlled herself and been pleasantly surprised that Darrell had turned out to be a sweet guy and a great date. After considering all the rating categories they'd come up with, Bryn had finally awarded Darrell with a total of twenty-two stars. Not bad considering that twenty-five was comparable to a handsome knight on a white horse.

Emma leaned over to see Cassidy's iPad to go over their checklist again. She was tempted to rate Isaac with top honors by giving him twenty-five stars simply because he had been such a great date. But to be fair to her friends, she wanted to do this right. "Hmm . . ." She carefully studied the list.

1. Promptness
2. Politeness
3. Respectfulness
4. Appearance
5. Fun

"Let's see . . . Well, I guess all the guys should get five stars for promptness," she said. "Since they all arrived together and on time."

"Yes, but were they always prompt?" Bryn countered. "Coming from the refreshment table, bathroom breaks, and whatever, did Isaac ever keep you waiting?"

Emma thought about it. "No, I'd still have to give him five stars. And I'll give him four stars for politeness. That's because I caught him gaping at Devon's cleavage once. So I guess I can only give him four stars for respectfulness too—since that was disrespectful to me. And I'll only give him four stars for appearance since his pants really were all wrong for Mr. Knightley. But he tried. I will give him five stars for fun."

"That's a total of twenty-two," Cassidy told her.

Emma shrugged. "How about you, Cass? How would you rate your date with Mr. Scarecrow?"

Cassidy grinned. "That's easy. Russell gets twenty-five."

"Five stars all across?" Bryn looked skeptical.

"It's true," Cassidy argued. "Russell was the perfect date."

"What about all that sneezing and wheezing?" Bryn asked.

"He couldn't help that. And you could say he suffered like that for me since I needed a scarecrow to go with my Dorothy. Besides, the pill your grandmother gave him cleared it all up before the dance." Cassidy nodded. "Yes, I'd say my scarecrow was just about perfect."

"So are you in love?" Abby asked in a teasing tone.

"No way." Cass laughed. "Not yet anyway. How about you, Abby? I thought I saw stars in your eyes tonight. *Are you in love?*"

Abby giggled. "Kent is awesome, and I would venture to say that I'm in serious *like*."

"And how would you rate your date?" Bryn asked curiously.

"Well, I can't think of a single thing Kent did wrong." Abby sighed. "Seriously, he was so supportive when Devon acted like she wanted to kill me. And he made her meanness almost seem like it was part of *The Hunger Games*. Like she was one of the competitors who was out to get us. Really, it was kinda fun. Anyway, I have to give him a twenty-five too."

"Too bad we don't have kissing on the list," Bryn teased. "How would you and Emma rate your dates in that category?" She pointed to Abby first.

"Hmm . . ." Abby closed her eyes and sighed dreamily. "I'd have to give him a five there too." She opened her eyes. "Just don't tell my dad."

They all laughed.

"How about you, Em?" Bryn pointed at Emma now.

"I don't kiss and tell."

"You're no fun," Bryn told her.

Emma shrugged. "Well, I suppose he'd get a five there. Does that bring him up to twenty-seven points now? Second place to Kent since he'd now have thirty?"

"It's not a competition," Bryn reminded her.

"If it was, we could all guess who would come in last place," Abby said. "If Devon was here anyway. She'd give poor Leonard straight zeroes."

"No, she'd probably give him minuses," Bryn corrected.

"Speaking of Devon, what do you think happened to her?" Cassidy looked genuinely concerned. "I mean, we know she kind of disappeared at the dance, but we all assumed she'd gone home. But at the time, we didn't know she'd been drinking."

"I wonder how much she'd been drinking," Abby said.

"Do you think we should check on her?" Cassidy asked.

"She probably went home and passed out," Bryn suggested.

"I checked my phone already," Emma admitted as she reached for her phone again. "I thought she might've sent a message."

"Did she?"

"No." Emma looked at her phone. "Still nothing."

"Does she usually text you a lot?" Abby asked. "I mean, at times like this when she's, well, so ticked at everyone?"

"I actually kinda expected to hear from her hours ago," Emma confessed. "But maybe Bryn's right. Devon might've gone home and passed out." Emma didn't like thinking of Devon like that—it was so bizarre. But hearing about her drinking vodka at the dance was pretty strange too. What was wrong with Devon?

"Since we're on the subject of Devon." Bryn pursed her lips. "I think we should make a decision about her membership in the DG. I want to go on record as saying that I like Devon. But she's broken a lot of rules. And this whole sneaking vodka into the dance biz—and during our limo ride too—well, that is unacceptable."

"Northwood has a zero tolerance policy for alcohol and drugs," Cassidy reminded everyone. "Does everyone agree that the DG has the same?"

They all agreed.

"I feel bad." Abby's voice broke. "Like this is partly my fault. If I hadn't set Devon up with Leonard, maybe she wouldn't have—"

"Are you blaming yourself for Devon having vodka in her purse at the dance?" Bryn asked her. "Because—think about it—she had to have brought that with her before she even knew Leonard was her blind date. Where else could she have gotten it?"

They kicked this around for a while but were never quite able to agree on where and how Devon could have acquired the vodka. But they did agree it was stupid and wrong. "And not only wrong," Cassidy clarified. "Underage drinking is illegal and grounds for expulsion from Northwood."

"There's just one thing," Emma said. "We don't know for absolute certain that Devon had vodka or that she was drinking vodka. That's just what Leonard said. Not that I think he lied. But knowing Devon, well, it's possible she had a flask in her purse. It's also possible that it was filled with water and that she was just jerking his chain."

"I can imagine Devon doing that," Abby said. "She likes to jerk people around sometimes."

"Even so," Bryn argued, "Devon broke DG rules tonight. You guys know that. Do we just let her off? And if we let her off, how do we know it won't happen again? Or maybe she'll do something even worse."

"Or she might bring the whole DG down," Cassidy said sadly.

"I don't like playing the heavy," Bryn said, "but I think we should take a vote as to whether or not Devon can remain a member."

"I understand that we need to do this," Emma said, "but I feel like we need to talk to Devon first. It's not like this is a court of law or anything, but it seems only fair that she should get to defend herself."

"That seems fair," Cassidy said. "Like the point Emma made about the vodka. What if it was only water?"

"I agree," Abby told them. "I want to hear Devon's side before we vote."

Bryn sighed. "Fine. Let's wait then."

"Good." Emma let out a relieved sigh. Now she wanted to change the subject. Talking about Devon was too depressing. "Okay, is it just me, or did anyone else really feel like they could relate to their literary character tonight? I mean, I was going around and trying to make everyone happy. Arranging for a guy to dance with Devon—and then finding someone for Leonard. I was even sacrificing my time with Isaac to pacify Devon. Especially when she started hitting on him. Anyway, I really felt like I was Emma Woodhouse. I could relate to how she gets so busy trying to figure out everyone else's life that she completely neglects her own."

"So you felt neglected?" Bryn teased.

"I definitely felt distracted. But it got better eventually." She almost added "when Devon disappeared," but that seemed harsh. "I guess it was kind of like how everything changed for Emma at the end of the book."

"So what did you learn?" Cassidy asked.

"Learn?" Emma considered this. "Well, it's good to help others . . . but I guess you shouldn't help others so much that you ruin your own life."

"Ooh, that's a good lesson," Bryn told her.

"I could totally relate to my character too," Abby said. "Almost like I really was Katniss for a while. At first I thought it was just my imagination, but then Peeta—I mean Kent—started acting like we were in peril too. He was helping me hide and avoid Devon, making these strategies and stuff. At first it was kind of creepy since it really did feel like Devon was about to start a hair-pulling catfight, but then it was actually kind of exciting and fun. Isn't that weird?"

"So what did you learn?" Emma asked her.

"I'm not sure." Abby frowned. "But the most obvious thing was how it was a big mistake to get Leonard for Devon's blind date. I totally regretted it then and I still do now. And I plan to apologize to Devon. Not that she'll forgive me. I doubt she'll ever speak to me again."

"Which is one more reason to remove Devon from the DG," Bryn pointed out.

"But right now we're telling about our characters," Cassidy reminded her. "I actually felt a lot like Dorothy too. It was earlier tonight—before we went to the dance. I was really, really nervous about setting Bryn up with Darrell."

"That's true," Emma told them. "Cass was a basket case."

"Well, you should've been," Bryn pointed out. "That could've gone really, really wrong."

"Believe me, I know. Darrell had promised to make my life miserable if it did. And I felt pretty certain you would hate me too, Bryn. But Russell—my scarecrow—reminded me of how brave Dorothy was. He gave me this great little pep talk and I decided that if everything fell apart, I would do whatever it took to put it all back together again."

"As it turned out, you must've done a pretty good job since Bryn gave Darrell twenty-two stars," Abby declared.

"So what did you learn?" Emma asked her.

"That just like Dorothy, I will never get where I'm going without a little help from my friends."

"That's good," Emma told her. "Sometimes you try to be so strong and do things on your own. It's good you realize that you need us."

"And tonight I needed Russell too."

"Okay," Bryn said eagerly. "My turn to tell you about how I felt like Daisy tonight. And I really did. It was so weird. There was this moment in Grandpa's pool room—after I realized who my blind date was—that I was so indignant and angry. Kind of how Devon acted. And I got this image of Daisy Buchanan rejecting Jay Gatsby because he wasn't wealthy enough. And I realized what a huge mistake she made back then. If only she hadn't done that, everyone's life would've gone so differently. People wouldn't have had their hearts broken, people wouldn't have died. But all because Daisy thought she wanted something more, she ruined everything. Does that make sense?"

"Makes sense to me," Emma said quietly. Not only did it make sense to her, it sounded painfully like Devon. Just like Daisy Buchanan, Devon always seemed to think she deserved something better. She always wanted something more. Devon wanted the perfect boyfriend. She wanted to have "fun." She wanted her parents to get back together. Sometimes she wanted Emma to be her best friend—and at other times she wanted Bryn. She wanted to be prettier. She wanted to have more money, to have a better house, to have her own car. Devon wanted and wanted and wanted. And a lot of her wanting seemed to lead to bad choices. Stupid decisions that could ruin everything for her.

Abby woke up early on Saturday. At first she was confused, trying to remember where she was and why, but as her eyes adjusted to the semidarkness, she realized it was only Bryn's basement. The rest of her friends appeared to still be soundly sleeping. Not surprising, since they'd stayed up until nearly 3:00 watching a DVD. She and Bryn had shared the sofa bed, and now Abby was reluctant to get up and disturb her slumbering friend.

So she remained motionless, staring at a sliver of gray light coming through the high narrow window and thinking. She was dismayed to discover she felt even more guilty about Devon this morning than she had last night. If she hadn't set up Devon with a date that she knew was all wrong, the whole evening would've gone so much better. For everyone. And now, if Devon was officially out of the DG, which seemed likely, it was partly Abby's fault. Maybe even mostly.

She wished there was a way to undo the damage. And maybe there was. Abby started to make a plan. To start with, she would attempt to reach out to Devon today. She would admit that she'd tried to sabotage her, and she would apologize to her. And if Devon would listen, Abby would encourage her to mend fences with the other girls. Perhaps they could have an emergency DG meeting. Then Abby could plead Devon's case with the other girls and, if necessary, beg them to accept Devon back. If they refused, Abby could threaten to quit the club. In fact, that was probably the best thing to do.

Abby knew that her dad would be disappointed in her if he knew what was going on with her. First of all, he'd be disappointed that she'd let down a friend. But perhaps even more than that, he'd be disappointed if he knew what kind of friend Devon actually was. Dad didn't really know Devon. And if he did know her, he would not approve. He would lecture Abby about being influenced by her peers. He would warn her to beware of the "company she kept." And to be honest, he would be partially right. But not totally.

Abby had always considered herself a strong and moral person. However, if she was being completely honest, she had to admit that she'd compromised her standards when she'd invited Leonard to be Devon's date. Not because there was anything wrong with Leonard. Well, besides being a little bit nerdy. The problem was that *Abby had known better*. Her conscience had warned her. But she had not listened.

A chiming phone caught her attention now. It wasn't hers, but she wondered if she should get up and answer it.

"My phone," Emma said groggily, fumbling around where she and Cassidy were sharing the queen-size air mattress on the floor and finally muttering hello as she got up to wander toward the bathroom.

Both Bryn and Cassidy were still fast asleep, so Abby

decided to get up and get a drink of water. She was just finishing it when Emma emerged from the bathroom. "That was my mom," she whispered.

"Oh." Abby nodded as she dropped the paper cup into the trash.

"She's worried about Devon," Emma said in a slightly urgent voice.

"Devon? What do you mean?"

"Mom said that Devon's mom called this morning. Apparently she'd gone off for the weekend with her boyfriend. Anyway, I guess her neighbor called and told her that the front door to their house was wide open early this morning. They wanted to make sure everything was okay."

"Huh?" Abby was confused.

"So Devon's mom called my mom to make sure Devon was there."

"Was where?"

"With me. Apparently Devon's mom thought Devon was spending the weekend at my house."

"Oh." Abby nodded, slowly taking this in. "But Devon went home, right?"

"That's what I thought. But apparently she's not answering her phone, and my mom was worried too."

"What did you tell your mom?"

"That I'd have Devon call her mom." Emma bit her lip. "But now I'm wondering why the front door would be wide open."

"She forgot to close it?" Abby ventured, but even as she said this a bad feeling ran through her. "Do you think she's okay?"

"I don't know." Emma was pulling on clothes now. "But I'm going to find out."

"I want to go with you," Abby told her.

As the two of them were hurrying to dress, the other two woke up. Emma quickly filled them in, and everyone agreed they should go together to Devon's house. Bryn's mom had set out some breakfast things for the girls, as well as a note explaining that they'd left for an early golf date.

"Good, I won't have to explain this to my parents," Bryn said as she grabbed a muffin. "You guys help yourselves."

"Let's take some for Devon too," Abby suggested as she wrapped several things in a napkin.

As Bryn drove them to Devon's house, the girls speculated on reasons the front door could have been open and why Devon wasn't answering her phone. The more they talked, the wilder the possibilities seemed to become.

"I wonder whose car that is in the driveway?" Emma pointed to a beat-up–looking blue car as Bryn pulled in front of the house.

"Maybe we should call the police," Cassidy said nervously.

"That's silly," Bryn told her. "What would we tell them? That the door is open and there's a car in the driveway?"

"But what if something happened to her?" Cassidy asked.

"Yeah," Emma added, "what if someone broke in to Devon's house? What if she's been . . . well, hurt or something?"

"Come on," Bryn urged. "There are four of us. It's broad daylight. We all have our phones. Let's peek inside and if anything looks the slightest bit suspicious we'll call the cops. Okay?"

"Yeah," Abby agreed. "Let's go."

With Bryn and Abby leading the way, the girls went up to the house and peered inside. "Hello?" Bryn called loudly. "Devon, are you in there?"

"Hello?" Abby yelled. "Devon?"

"Huh?" a groggy-sounding male voice answered.

"Who's that?" Bryn looked at Abby with wide eyes.

Abby peeked around the corner to see a guy sitting up on the couch in the living room. It looked as if they'd woken him up. "Who *is* that?" she hissed back at Bryn. "And what's he doing here?"

"What's going on?" Emma demanded loudly. "Who's in there?"

"That's Brandon West," Bryn declared.

"No way," Emma said.

"It is," Abby confirmed as she watched him staggering through the trashed living room, gathering up his shoes and a letterman jacket from Jackson High. Brandon West had gone to Northwood a couple years back, but he'd been expelled. According to rumor, his expulsion was the result of a long list of infractions. Everyone knew that Brandon West was trouble.

"What are *you* doing here?" Emma demanded as she pushed past the others to confront the tall, blond guy.

Brandon looked down at Emma with a startled expression. "I—uh—I was here with—uh—what's her name?"

"Devon?" Emma said.

"Yeah." He nodded as he shoved his foot into a shoe. "Devon." He stood up straight, then gave them a lopsided grin. "We were partying. Hey, you girls here to party too?"

"You're disgusting," Emma told him.

"Where's Devon?" Abby asked.

He shrugged, reaching for his other shoe.

"Keep him here," Abby told Bryn and Cassidy as she grabbed Emma's hand. "Let's go make sure Devon's okay."

They eventually found Devon in her mom's bedroom, face-down on the bed and wearing a very rumpled Juliet dress. Like the rest of the house, this room was a mess too. *"Devon!"* Emma called out as she shook the lifeless girl. *"Wake up!"*

"Is she dead?" Abby asked in horror.

"No." Emma let Devon flop back onto the bed. "I saw her eyes fluttering." She shook her head. "And I smelled her breath. Eww!"

Abby took Devon by the shoulders now, giving her a good, hard shake. "Devon, wake up!" she said loudly.

"Is Devon okay?" Bryn yelled from the living room. "Should we call 911?"

"No," Emma called out as she left the room. "Not yet, anyway."

"Come on, Devon," Abby urged. "Wake up or we're going to call 911."

Devon's eyes slowly opened. "Go 'way," she muttered.

"No," Abby told her. "You're a mess and we're not leaving you like this."

Devon closed her eyes again, letting out a sound that was part growl and part groan.

"I have exactly what she needs," Emma said as she returned to the bedroom.

Abby looked up in time to see Emma armed with a full glass of water. The next thing she knew, Emma tossed it right into Devon's face. Poor Devon sat up, sputtering and gasping and blinking. Meanwhile Emma just laughed.

"You idiots!" Devon swore at them. "Just leave me alone!"

"Get up," Abby commanded Devon, pulling her by both hands. "Let's walk you around and make sure you're okay."

"Don't wanna walk," Devon said as they got her to her feet.

"Shut up and walk," Emma told her.

Abby gave Emma a warning glance. "We don't have to be mean," she whispered as they guided Devon out of the room and down the hallway.

"Yeah," Devon grumbled. "Don't be mean."

"That's right," Emma told her. "Looks like you've done a good job of being mean to yourself."

"Is she okay?" Cassidy asked when they finally made it to the living room.

"I wouldn't say she's okay," Abby told them. "But she's alive."

"So I can go?" Brandon asked in a cocky tone.

"Who needs you?" Emma told him.

He laughed, slung his jacket over his shoulder, and sauntered out.

"What a jerk," Bryn said.

"Yeah." Cassidy pointed at Devon. "Why are you hanging with someone like that?"

"And why are you drinking?" Bryn held an empty whiskey bottle in front of her face.

"What is wrong with you?" Emma asked her.

"I—uh—I feel sick," Devon muttered.

"Get her to the bathroom," Bryn yelled. "Hurry, before she hurls!"

Abby and Emma ran Devon to the bathroom, making it to the toilet in time for Devon to collapse and vomit violently.

Abby looked at Emma. "What a mess."

"Did you see the house?" Emma quietly asked her.

Abby nodded.

"Why did she do this?" Emma asked with balled fists. "Why is she so stupid?"

Abby shrugged as she watched Devon continuing to throw up. Then she went over to the sink, found a hand towel, and soaked it in cold water before slowly wringing it out. When Devon had stopped vomiting, Abby handed the damp towel to her. "Here, clean off your face," she said gently.

Devon let out a little sob as she wiped her face on the wet towel.

"I can't take this," Emma declared as she stormed out of the bathroom. "Devon disgusts me."

"Can you stand up?" Abby asked Devon.

"I—uh—I think so," Devon said in a hoarse voice.

Abby helped her to her feet before flushing the toilet, trying not to gag herself. She lowered the seat, closed the lid, and helped Devon sit down. "Feel better?"

"A little." Devon was still pressing the damp towel to her head.

Abby wanted to ask Devon why she'd done this to herself. But at the same time she figured Devon wasn't ready to answer that question yet. She looked down at Devon's disheveled, dirty clothes, noticing that she'd gotten vomit on her sad-looking Juliet dress as well as in her hair. "You could probably use a shower."

Devon nodded.

"Do you think you're strong enough?"

Devon shrugged. But the smell was so nasty that Abby decided to insist. After a bit of struggling, she helped Devon undress and got her into the shower, helping her to wash her hair.

"What are you doing?" Bryn demanded, sticking her head into the steamy bathroom with a concerned expression.

"Cleaning her up," Abby explained as she reached for a towel.

"But what if she was—well, what if Brandon did something to her?"

"Huh?" Abby stared at Bryn. "What do you mean?"

"Like what if he did something like—"

"Don't worry, Bryn!" Devon grabbed the towel from Abby. "I'm fine. Brandon and I didn't do anything."

"Besides getting wasted?" Bryn asked.

Devon scowled as she wrapped the towel around her.

"And trashing your mom's house?" Bryn added.

"Whatever!" Devon snarled. "That's my problem anyway."

Abby got another towel to wrap around Devon's dripping hair, and in that same moment, Devon turned to Abby with grateful eyes. "Thanks," she muttered.

"Yeah . . ." Abby nodded as she dropped the Juliet dress into the full sink to soak.

"Cassidy is looking up hangover remedies," Bryn quietly told Abby. "But mostly they just say drink water and take aspirin."

Abby opened the medicine cabinet above the sink. Finding a bottle of aspirin, she shook a couple out and then filled a glass of water. She handed them to Devon. "Here, take this."

Devon looked uncertain but did as Abby said.

"What if I barf again?" Devon asked as she handed the glass back to her.

Abby shrugged. "Let's get you to your room." But as they went out, she grabbed the bathroom wastebasket. "You can have this in case you throw up."

Abby helped Devon pull on some warm-ups and got her into her bed, making sure to keep the wastebasket nearby.

"Why're you being nice to me?" Devon asked weakly.

Abby shrugged as she put an extra pillow beneath Devon's still-damp head.

"The others hate me, don't they?"

"They don't hate you," Abby said gently, "but they don't understand you. To be honest, I don't either."

Devon rolled her eyes, then shut them.

Abby took in a deep breath. "But I want to apologize to you," she said quickly.

Devon's eyes flickered open. "Why?"

"For setting you up with Leonard. I know that was wrong. I know it ruined the dance for you. And I want you to know that I'm truly sorry."

Devon let out a little sigh, then closed her eyes again.

"I hope you can forgive me . . . someday."

Devon said nothing as Abby gathered the damp towels. Feeling guilty and sad, Abby carried the dirty laundry out through the living room. There, much to her surprise, she discovered the other girls were picking up the pieces of last night's party. "I thought you guys went home," Abby said as she stared in wonder.

"Some of us wanted to," Cassidy admitted as she carried a bag of trash into the kitchen.

"But it was too disgusting to leave like this." Emma held up a dirty T-shirt with a wrinkled nose.

Abby added it to her towels and took them to the laundry room. Then she joined her friends and together they cleaned the trashed house. She took regular breaks to go check on Devon, coaxing her to drink some Sierra Mist.

After a couple of hours, the house was greatly improved and the other girls were ready to leave. But Abby insisted on staying.

"I already called my mom," she explained. "She'll pick me up later."

Emma frowned. "I should be the one who stays with Devon," she told Abby. "But I'm still so furious at her . . . I can hardly stand to be in the same room with her."

"It's okay," Abby assured her. "I'm staying because I *want* to."

"Call if you need help," Cassidy told her.

After the others left, Abby continued to straighten and scrub. She started with the bathroom, which didn't appear to have been deeply cleaned for ages, then eventually moved on to the kitchen. It felt good to stay busy, and on some level, she felt she was making up for Devon's bad blind date, which might've been part of what led to Devon's bad choices. Sure, Abby knew that all this was not her personal fault. Like Emma and the others had so clearly pointed out, Devon had made her own decisions to mess up last night. But if it made Abby feel better to help Devon, well, what did that hurt?

It wasn't until later in the day that Devon felt well enough to get out of bed and eat some chicken noodle soup that Abby heated in the microwave for her.

"You don't have to stick around," Devon said as she nibbled on a saltine cracker.

"I want to."

"Because you feel guilty?" Devon's smudged eye makeup made her resemble a raccoon, and her skin looked pale and drawn.

"Maybe." Abby rinsed the soup bowl in the sink, then set it in the dishwasher.

"For the record, I did *not* want you guys to clean up." Devon scowled darkly.

"Why not?" Abby closed the dishwasher with a bang.

"Because I wanted my mom to come home to the mess."

"Seriously?" Abby stared at her in disbelief.

"She deserved it."

"Why?" Abby sat down across the table from her.

"Because she's abandoning me." Devon's eyes were filling with tears. "Just like my dad did. My mom is going to marry Rodney."

"Just because she marries Rodney doesn't mean she's abandoning you."

"Yes, it does!" Devon slammed her fist onto the table. "Rodney hates me. And I hate him. Mom will choose him over me. I know it."

"Oh . . ." Abby tried to wrap her head around this. She could not imagine her parents ever abandoning her, or divorcing each other, or falling in love with someone else who hated her. It was inconceivable. Sometimes she'd actually wished they didn't care so much. Like even when she'd told Mom why she was here—saying she was helping a sick friend without going into all the details—Mom had wanted to come over and help too.

"So I wanted to show her," Devon continued. "I wanted her to see *this* is what happens when you treat your kids like this—when you abandon them." Tears were streaming down her cheeks now.

"Is that why you got drunk?"

Devon nodded, wiping her tears with her hands. "I wanted to hurt her—like she hurt me."

"Oh."

"And I wanted to show her," Devon sobbed, "that I still—I still need a mom."

Abby went over to Devon, and leaning over, she wrapped her arms around Devon's shoulders and hugged her tightly as she cried. "I'm so sorry." Abby choked back her own tears. "I'm really, really sorry."

Eventually the two girls made their way to the living room, sitting across from each other on the couch in silence. Abby felt sorry for Devon but didn't know what more to say or what more to do. However, she did have some questions. "Do you mind if I ask how all this happened, Devon?"

"All what?"

"The alcohol last night . . . How you got home from the dance . . . How Brandon wound up asleep on your couch . . . How the place got trashed . . ." Abby grimaced to remember the mess that had been here. "I mean, I'm just curious how something like that happens."

Devon made a crooked smile. "Truthfully?"

Abby nodded. "Yeah. What happened?"

"The truth is I can't remember everything. But I do remember finding my mom's stash of booze, and I remember setting this place up for a party."

"Why?" Abby frowned. "Who did you think you'd party with? The DG?"

Devon shrugged. "I don't know. I guess I wasn't really thinking straight."

"And you took alcohol to the dance. Why?"

"Because I was so mad at my mom."

Abby tried to understand this. "Isn't that kind of like trying to hurt someone else by knocking yourself in the head with a hammer?"

Devon sighed as she reached up to her forehead. "Yeah, it kinda feels like that too."

"So how did Brandon end up here?" Abby pressed on.

"He was Jennie Preston's date last night. He wasn't having

such a good time with her. We kinda met up outside . . . and we shared some drinks."

"Okay . . ."

"Then he offered to take me home. Or maybe I asked him for a ride. It's kinda fuzzy. Anyway, after we got here he saw that I had this little party all laid out, and he called some of his friends from Jackson." She held up her hands. "That's about all I remember specifically."

Abby shook her head. "Do you realize how dangerous that could've been? You drink until you pass out, you leave your house wide open all night long. Anything could've happened to you." Abby felt almost like her dad was doing the talking for her—and yet she knew they were words that needed to be spoken. "Do you even get that?"

Devon frowned. "Not so much last night . . . Maybe now I do."

"You were totally wasted," Abby continued. "Do you know that people can die from alcohol poisoning?"

"I kinda felt like I was dying this morning," Devon admitted.

Seeing that Devon was on the verge of tears again, Abby controlled the urge to continue blasting her. "It's just that I care about you," she said finally. "If you care about yourself, you won't pull something like this again."

"Yeah . . . probably not." But now she looked up with a mischievous twinkle in her bloodshot eyes. "But you never know."

• ● ● ● •

When Abby finally called her mom to pick her up, it was after 4:00. Naturally, Mom was concerned and curious as she drove home. At first Abby tried to play the whole thing down. No way did she want her parents to know that Devon had nearly drunk herself to death. Because that's what Abby felt like Devon had been trying to do—whether it was conscious or not. But Abby did tell Mom about how messed up things were at Devon's house. "The truth is, I didn't really like Devon very much before," she confessed. "I didn't care about what was going on in her life. I just wanted her to straighten up. You know?"

Mom nodded without speaking.

"But now I actually care about her. And if I can, I want to help her."

"At the very least you proved yourself to be a good friend to her," Mom said as they got home.

"I hope I can be a good influence on her," Abby said as they got out of the car. "I know Dad's worried that my friends could influence me too much. But I really hope that I can influence Devon."

"I'm sure that if anyone can, it would be you, sweetie." Mom gave her a sideways hug as they went into the house.

Abby wished she felt as certain as Mom did. The truth was, she had her doubts. Seeing Devon like she'd seen her today was eye-opening on many levels. Yes, she felt genuinely sorry for Devon, and the situation with her mom was disturbing and sad. But at the same time, Abby felt seriously concerned. Devon was as unpredictable as a loaded gun, so filled with hurt and anger and confusion. Abby felt sure this girl could easily self-destruct. Sometimes it almost seemed as if Devon wanted to blow up her own life. And what if—in her carelessness—she took others along with her? Perhaps Bryn was right. Maybe it was time to remove Devon from the DG, to separate themselves from her. But what would happen to

Devon then? First her dad abandons her, then her mom, and now her friends. What might Devon do?

As Abby considered the grim possibilities, she felt seriously guilty for even considering this. More than that, she felt responsible. There was no doubt that Devon needed friends right now. Good, dependable, stable, responsible friends. More than that, *Devon needed God*. If there was any way Abby could convey this to Devon, it would be well worth the effort—and the risk.

So what *is* the point of the DG?" Cassidy asked. All the DG members except Devon had gotten together for an "emergency" meeting at Costello's on Saturday night. Abby had just made a statement about how the DG wasn't only about dating and guys. Sure, maybe that had been the motivation at the beginning—although not for Cassidy—but perhaps the other girls were seeing it differently now too.

"It's about friendship," Emma said dismally.

"And about being a club," Bryn added.

"All I'm saying," Abby continued, "is that Devon *needs* us. She needs friends. Probably more now than ever. We can't just toss her aside."

"But what about our rules?" Bryn demanded. "Do we bend and break them for Devon?"

Abby shrugged. "I don't know."

"Does Devon even *want* to be in the DG anymore?" Emma asked. "I mean, she sure doesn't act like it."

"I don't think Devon knows what she wants," Abby told them. "I think she's hurting and confused. And I think if we dump her, we'll be partially responsible for Devon's . . ." She sighed, holding up her hands in a helpless gesture.

"For Devon's *what*?" Cassidy pressed. How serious was this for Devon?

"Crashing and burning," Abby said quietly.

"That's a lot of responsibility to throw on our shoulders," Bryn pointed out.

"Maybe we never should've started this club in the first place," Abby declared.

"Maybe we should end it now," Cassidy said sadly.

The table got quiet and the four of them looked at each other.

"But it's been fun." Bryn's mouth twisted to one side.

"Yeah," Emma added. "I've enjoyed getting to know you guys better."

"I've liked it too," Cassidy confessed.

"So what do we do?" Abby asked them. "Because I mean what I said—if you kick Devon out, I'm going too."

"Back to my earlier question," Emma said. "Does Devon even want to be part of the DG anymore? It seemed to me that she was trying to blow us all off when she came to the dance with vodka in her purse. She might've even wanted to get kicked out of the school."

"I don't think that was why she did that," Abby told them.

"Then why did she do it?" Cassidy asked.

Abby looked torn. "I don't know how much to say."

"You'd better say something," Cassidy encouraged. "Right now you're the only defense Devon has."

"And she definitely needs it," Bryn told her.

"Normally, I'd be the one defending her," Emma said, "but I've just about had it with her." Emma made an exaggerated sigh. "And I get to go home to her after this. She's staying at my house until her mom gets home."

"How's she doing?" Cassidy asked.

"She's okay, I guess. But she's barricaded herself up in the guest room and isn't talking to anyone." Emma shrugged. "Suits me fine."

Cassidy pointed at Abby again. "Anyway, it's up to you. Either you shed some light on this mess with Devon or we're done here."

"And then your club shrinks to three members," Abby reminded her.

"We can get new members," Bryn told her. "I already know of several girls who would love to be included."

"Maybe that would be good," Emma said eagerly.

"Fine." Abby looked hurt as she stood. "If that's how you want it."

"Wait." Cassidy put a hand on Abby's arm. "You still haven't told us what's up with Devon or why she did what she did."

"And don't try to take the blame again," Bryn warned Abby. "We already told you that Devon makes her own choices. Just because she was ticked over her blind date is not an excuse to turn into a complete idiot."

"Right." Abby sat down again. "Devon might get mad at me for telling you this." She looked around the table. "But since you're all members of the DG, I think I can trust you. Right?"

They all seemed to agree, encouraging Abby to continue.

"Devon was really upset over her mom running off with her boyfriend again this weekend. She's certain they're going to get married. And she's equally certain they'll abandon her.

Just like her dad abandoned her. And I'm sure she thinks we'll abandon her too. So I'm guessing she just decided to blow up her own life before someone else did it for her."

Emma nodded. "That sounds about right. Like how Devon thinks."

"Wow, that's sad," Cassidy admitted. "I didn't know she was so desperate." Cassidy felt guilty now. She'd been determined to be a better friend to Devon, but she'd gotten so busy and caught up with their recent blind date stuff that she'd sort of forgotten.

"That is kinda rough," Bryn said with a furrowed brow. "I didn't realize Devon's mom was thinking of remarrying."

"Apparently she is," Abby told them. "And she'd taken off without even letting Devon know. That hurt Devon's feelings."

"That's true," Emma confirmed. "My mom said pretty much the same thing. In fact, she's kinda ticked at Devon's mom now. It wasn't fair to Devon."

"So Devon is hurt that her mom's taken off like that, worried that she's being abandoned . . ." Cassidy was putting the pieces together. "And then her date turns out to be a disappointment, and maybe she feels sabotaged—like we ganged up against her or something."

"So she throws caution and common sense to the wind," Bryn added, "and winds up in a big mess."

"Which hurt her more than it hurt anyone else," Abby finished for them. "Now the question is—do we want to hurt her even more?"

"I think it's time to put it to a vote," Cassidy told them. "And remember rule number ten. It takes a unanimous vote to either admit or remove a member of the DG." She looked around the table. "All in favor of removing Devon from the DG, raise your hand."

No hands went up. All of them let out a relieved sigh.

"So it's settled." Cassidy closed the cover on her iPad. "Who wants to let Devon know?"

"Did she even know that she was about to get kicked out?" Bryn asked.

"Yes," Emma confessed with a sheepish expression. "I may have conveyed that bit of information to her before I left."

"Really?" Cassidy was surprised. "How did she take it?"

"She acted like she didn't care . . . but I could tell."

"What?"

Emma looked contrite. "That she was hurt."

"Poor Devon."

Emma held up her phone. "I can call her and let her know."

"Why don't we all let her know?" Abby suggested.

"Yeah, that's a good idea." Cassidy slid her iPad into her bag. "Let's go to Emma's right now."

• • • • •

While Cassidy drove the three other girls to Emma's house, she thought more about Devon's situation. She hoped that Devon hadn't been hurt enough to pull some other stupid stunt. As she parked her car, she decided that she was going to try a lot harder to convince Devon that her friendship was genuine.

They all got out and Emma led the way into the house.

"What's going on?" Emma's mom looked up from her computer with concern.

"We're here to talk to Devon," Emma explained in a no-nonsense tone.

Her mom smiled and nodded. "I haven't seen her. I assume she's still in the guest room."

Emma led the way and then knocked on the closed door at

the end of the hall. When Devon didn't answer, she opened the door and they all walked into the darkened room. Emma turned on the overhead light.

"What the—*Emma*?" Devon sat up, blinking in the brightness. "Can't a person have any privacy in this house?" Now she seemed to realize that Emma wasn't alone. "What's up?"

"We want to talk to you," Cassidy told her.

Devon shrugged. "Make yourselves at home."

Soon they were all settled on the bed and Cassidy explained how they had met to vote on whether or not Devon could remain a member of the DG. "But then we decided to bring the meeting to you." Cassidy pulled out her iPad as if she was going to take notes.

"It's because you broke so many rules," Emma told Devon. "And in all fairness, we could've kicked you out."

Devon shrugged again. "So?"

"Do you want to get kicked out?" Abby asked.

Devon folded her arms across her front. "I don't care."

"I think you *do* care," Emma challenged her. "I think you care a lot, but you don't want to admit it. You don't want to ruin your tough-chick persona."

Devon glared at her.

"Hey, if you don't want to be part of the DG, maybe we should just forget the whole thing," Bryn said in a slightly snooty tone.

"Why doesn't everyone take a nice, deep breath," Cassidy said quietly.

"Yeah." Abby nodded. "We didn't come here to attack Devon."

"Sure could've fooled me." Devon pressed her lips tightly together. "Almost feels like you guys came here to lynch me or something." Now she barely smiled. "And to be honest, I wouldn't blame you a bit."

"Really?" Emma looked shocked.

"Yeah." Devon let out a long, sad sigh. "I'm sorry, okay? I really blew it. It was totally stupid to start drinking like that yesterday. I'm not sure you guys care, but I didn't do it to hurt any of you. I'm not totally sure why I did it. I mean, I was mad at my mom. But what I did hurt me a whole lot more than it hurt her. She'll probably never even know what an idiot I was or how sick I got." Devon snickered. "Well, until she notices that her liquor stash has been raided." Devon looked from girl to girl. "But I really am sorry. And I deserve to be kicked out of the DG. I figured you already voted to get rid of me."

"We voted," Cassidy told her.

"To keep you," Abby added.

"Thanks to Abby's brilliant defense," Bryn told Devon. "If you ever need an attorney, old Abs is the one to get."

Devon smiled. "Thanks, you guys."

"But you have to promise us you won't do that again," Cassidy said suddenly. This wasn't something the DG had actually agreed upon, but she knew her friends would back her. "And you can't keep on breaking the rules either."

"That's right," Bryn said. "Just because we're giving you another chance doesn't mean we won't kick you out if you pull a stunt like that again."

"Trust me." Devon rubbed her head. "I never want to do anything like that again. I've never felt so sick in my life. I honestly thought I was going to die—I wanted to die!"

Cassidy started to giggle now.

"What's so funny?" Devon demanded.

"I just remembered something," Cassidy said between giggles.

"What is it?" Devon looked mad.

"Last night we were all talking about the various funny ways we could relate to our literary characters—you know, the ones we'd dressed up as. And it just hit me that you must've really related to Juliet too—because you went home and *poisoned yourself*!" Cassidy laughed nervously. "But sheesh, Devon, that was taking it way too far. I'm so glad you didn't succeed."

Pretty soon they were all laughing and joking about it—even Devon started to smile.

"But seriously," Emma told Devon in a stern tone. "If you ever do that again—no matter what the DG says—I am going to walk away from you. I refuse to stand by and watch my friend poisoning herself like that. *Do you understand?*"

Devon nodded somberly.

"I'm with Emma on that," Abby told her. "Our school has zero tolerance and I'm going to have to stick with them on it. Never again, Devon."

The others backed Abby and Emma, and Devon promised them that she wouldn't do it again. "If I could turn back the clock I would. It was totally stupid."

"And dangerous," Cassidy reminded her.

"And I'm sorry," Devon began slowly, "for how I acted last night at the dance too. I know I was kind of inebriated and I'm not completely sure of all that I said or did, but I realize that I might've spoiled the evening for some of you. And I'm really, really sorry."

They talked about it a little more and everyone agreed that they had forgiven her.

"Hopefully our next date will be better," Devon said.

"Speaking of that, what are our plans for our next date?" Bryn asked the others.

Several different ideas were tossed around, discussed, and argued over. Finally, Cassidy got a new idea. "What about a double date?"

"A double date?"

"You know, where two couples go out together," Cassidy told them.

"But there are only five of us," Abby pointed out. "That's not an even number. How can we each have a double date? Or does someone go out twice?"

"Maybe we need to admit a new member," Bryn suggested.

"Felicia Ruez would like to be part of the DG," Emma told them. "I never told her about the club, but she's been watching us and seems to know that we're up to something. She's asked me about it several times."

They discussed Felicia for a while, finally agreeing that she was a sweet, dependable girl and might make a good addition to the DG. A vote was taken and Felicia was unanimously accepted.

"That is, if she's really interested," Cassidy pointed out.

"I'll find out on Monday," Emma offered.

"So our next project will be a double date," Cassidy confirmed as she finished her notes on her iPad.

"But not a blind date," Devon said with uncertainty. "Right?"

"Right," Bryn agreed. "No more blind dates, thank you very much."

"I just want to say that I think the DG is about a whole lot more than Dating Games," Cassidy told them. "And I think that everyone here agrees with that."

"Absolutely," Emma said. "It's about our friendships."

"That's right," Abby reminded them. "If we don't stay strong in our friendships, the DG will disintegrate anyway."

Cassidy stuck her fist into the center of the circle of girls. "Here's to us, and here's to the DG." They all bumped fists in agreement. "Here's to friends!"

KEEP READING

for a sneak peek of

The Dating Games #3:

DOUBLE DATE

• THE DATING GAMES •

By Monday morning, Cassidy Banks had some serious doubts about Felicia Ruez—or more specifically, Felicia's *reputation*. Cassidy rarely paid attention to school gossip, but the stories she'd heard lately seemed to be jiving with the new image that Felicia was presenting.

Cassidy was the first to admit that of all the girls in the Dating Games club (aka the DG), she was by far the most conservative. So it hadn't escaped her notice that Felicia had recently undergone some kind of makeover—a redo that made Felicia look totally hot. Hot in a way that suggested she was going after some serious male attention.

But Cassidy didn't get it. After all, Felicia had always been exceptionally pretty—some even compared her to Penélope Cruz—and in Cassidy's opinion Felicia did not need to wear sexy clothes or flashy hair and bold makeup to turn guys' heads. They were already looking.

This fact had been driven home in Cassidy's Algebra II class just this morning. Poor Marcus Zimmerman couldn't take his eyes off Felicia as he came into the classroom today, so much so that he didn't notice a stray chair in the aisle and wound up toppling right over it, causing the class to roar with laughter. Naturally, Marcus made a quick recovery, feigning a dramatic bow as if he'd purposely choreographed the whole thing for their entertainment.

But Cassidy felt certain his accident was a result of Felicia's short-short skirt and low-cut top. And she suspected it was only a matter of time before Felicia was called down to the dean's office and reminded of the school's rigid dress code. Northwood Academy had put an end to the dreaded school uniforms several years back, but as a result the dress code was firmly enforced. At least it used to be.

"We need to talk," Cassidy said quietly to Emma Parks, accosting her friend as she emerged from the restroom and pulling her aside.

Emma's fair eyebrows shot up. "What? Are you breaking up with me?" she teased.

"Ha ha," Cassidy said with sarcasm, then lowered her voice. "Did you talk to Felicia yet?"

"No, but I asked her to meet me in the cafeteria to—"

"Well, hold your horses."

"What?"

"I've changed my mind."

"Huh?" Emma's brow creased in confusion. "Whatd'ya mean?"

"I know we all voted to let Felicia into the DG last week," Cassidy began quietly, "but I—"

"I already told Felicia to meet me at lunch today."

"You need to cool your jets." Cassidy tugged Emma away from a girl who looked overly interested in their conversation.

"But Felicia is really hoping she's in," Emma persisted. "And we need her in order to have an even number of girls for our whole double date—"

"Maybe so. But I am rescinding my vote."

"Rescinding?" Emma frowned. "Meaning you're backing out completely? You don't want Felicia in the DG at all? *Ever?*"

"That's right." Cassidy glanced around to be sure no one could overhear her. "I have reasons to believe Felicia isn't a good fit for the DG."

"What kind of reasons?"

"I'll tell the DG at lunch," Cassidy said. "I just wanted to be sure you hadn't given Felicia that green light yet."

Emma looked skeptical. "You haven't been listening to gossip, have you, Cass? I mean, that is so unlike you. But if you have, you better—"

"Hear me out at lunch, okay? I have to get to class now." As Cassidy scurried away, she felt slightly guilty. Was she overreacting? What if what she'd heard was wrong? But just as she thought this, she saw Felicia hurrying toward the English Department. That little yellow skirt was so short that Cassidy felt certain Felicia would be unable to pick up a pencil from the floor without exposing her rear end. Why in the world did Felicia think she needed to dress like that anyway? And why in the world hadn't the dean of students called Felicia into her office by now? What was this school coming to?

• • ● • •

Despite her earlier concerns, Cassidy started doubting herself by the time lunchtime arrived. Was she being too hasty about Felicia? Too judgmental? Gossipy even? As she entered the cafeteria, she knew that she didn't want to be that kind of girl. She despised gossip and was usually outspoken about those who indulged in that kind of meanness. But at the same time, she felt strangely protective of the DG. She didn't miss the irony here since she, of all the girls, had been the most skeptical about a dating club in the beginning.

But after all they'd been through and the friendships the five girls had formed, she felt compelled to preserve the integrity of the DG. To that end, she set her brown bag lunch aside and pulled out her iPad, opening up the rules that they'd written in September. She was perusing the document when the other girls started trickling up to their usual table.

Dating Games Club Rules

1. We will honor the secret membership of the DG.
2. We will be loyal to our fellow DG members.
3. We will help fellow DG members to find dates with good guys.
4. We will report back to the DG regarding our dates.
5. We will not be jealous over a fellow DG member's boyfriend.
6. We will never steal a fellow DG member's boyfriend.
7. We will abstain from sex on our DG dates.
8. We will not lie to the DG about what happens on our dates.
9. We will never let a boyfriend come between fellow DG members.
10. We will admit new DG members only by unanimous vote.

"Oh no," Bryn said in a teasing tone. "Cass is reading the DG rules again. Time for another little lecture?"

"I don't lecture anyone," Cassidy said defensively.

Emma set her tray down with a clunk and frowned. "Cass doesn't want Felicia in the DG," she chanted like a tattletale.

"I only said I'm having second thoughts," Cassidy clarified. "I rescinded my vote to buy us some time. We need to go over some things before we commit to another member."

"But we already voted," Bryn reminded her.

"Yes, but Emma hasn't told Felicia yet. And I'm calling an emergency meeting before she does," Cassidy informed them. "Any objections?"

"Not if you think it's really necessary." Bryn opened a packet of salad dressing.

"I do," Cassidy declared. "Think about it. Does anyone here want to induct a member who we'll regret having in the club later on?"

"Good point," Abby unwrapped a bean burrito. "I'd hate to have to kick someone out."

"And I have some questions about Felicia," Cassidy said quietly.

"I do too." Devon nodded eagerly as she opened a packet of ketchup.

"Really?" This was totally unexpected, but Cassidy tried to take it in stride. "Okay then. It's obvious we need to discuss this."

"Come on, you guys. What has poor Felicia done to deserve this kind of scrutiny?" Emma demanded. She pointed a finger at Cassidy. "And just so you know, I probably sounded like a stuck-up snob when I told her I couldn't talk right now. Even though I was the one who asked her to meet with me. I could tell by her expression that she thinks I'm just jerking her chain. And I don't blame her a bit. She probably won't even want to join now."

"So what's going on exactly?" Abby pointed her fork at Cassidy. "Why should we have second thoughts about Felicia?"

"I have some concerns," Cassidy started carefully. "It's partly about her appearance and part—"

"I know what this is," Bryn taunted. "Cassidy and Devon are worried that Felicia's too much competition."

"That's laughable." Devon pushed a strand of auburn hair over a shoulder, holding her chin high.

"And totally bogus." Cassidy held up her iPad like it held evidence. "Here's the deal. I don't think Felicia will *want* to comply with our rules."

"Which rules?" Abby asked with interest.

Cassidy scanned down the rules, stopping her finger on rule #7. "This one, for starters." She looked around uneasily. "But I'm not sure we should be having this meeting right now . . . in public. Especially not here in the cafeteria."

Now Emma leaned over, quietly reading the seventh rule loud enough for the others to hear. "We will abstain from sex on our DG dates." Her brow creased as she peered at Cassidy. "What are you saying about Felicia?"

"I'm saying I have reason for concern."

"Did Felicia tell you something that suggests that she can't comply with this rule?" Abby asked pointedly.

"No. But I overheard some girls in choir last week. They were talking about Felicia and—"

"This is about gossip?" Abby's dark brown eyes grew wide. "You of all people, Cass? You hate gossip."

"I know." Cassidy nodded contritely. "I do hate gossip. But it's not just that. I've noticed some things about Felicia—the way she's dressing and acting lately. Something has changed. Trust me, something's not right with that girl."

"I know exactly what Cassidy means," Devon declared. "Felicia is dressing like a hooker."

"Really, Devon." Emma used a scolding tone. "You should talk."

Devon pursed her lips with angry eyes. "What are you insinuating?"

"Well . . . you *used* to dress like a hooker. Before we made you—"

"I cannot believe you'd say something like that!"

"You know it's true. I still have some photos on my phone—"

"And I thought you were my friend!"

"Stop fighting." Cassidy held up a hand. "This is not why I brought this up right now."

"Are you trying to turn lunch into an official meeting?" Abby demanded. "Because I, for one, cannot do this. As soon as I finish eating, I need to get down to the gym to pick up my basketball uniform and get some—"

"This is the wrong place to talk about something like this," Bryn said. "If we need a real meeting, let's go to Costello's like we usually do."

"I agree," Devon said. "I move that we end this meeting."

"It's *not* a meeting," Cassidy pointed out.

"Whatever." Bryn tipped her head to a group of curious-looking girls standing nearby. "There are too many ears in here. Let's put a lid on it."

"But what am I supposed to tell Felicia?" Emma asked.

"Tell her to wait," Cassidy urged. "Just until we can meet and get this thing settled."

"Can everyone make it at 5:00?" Bryn asked.

"I might be late," Abby said with her mouth full. "We're starting practice this week. We don't usually quit until 5:00."

"How about 5:30 then?" Cassidy suggested. "And it can be a quick meeting."

"You really think we need this?" Bryn demanded.

"I don't," Emma told her.

"I do," Devon shot back at her. "Cassidy is absolutely right. I didn't want to say anything, but I have some questions about Felicia too. I've heard stuff like what Cassie is saying. We need to know what we're getting into . . . before we get into it."

"Well, that's very interesting, considering . . ." Bryn studied Devon with slightly narrowed eyes. "Hmm?"

Cassidy knew what Bryn was insinuating. She thought it was a little weird that Devon was speaking out against someone else's character like this. Especially since Devon had come so close to being thrown out of the DG only a few days ago. And although Cassidy appreciated the moral support in her quest to protect the DG, it wasn't too comforting that it only seemed to be coming from Devon. Siding with Devon on something like this was a bit disturbing.

Abby wadded up her napkin. "Okay then, I'll do my best to get to this meeting by 5:30. But you better make it worth my time. I mean, I do trust you, Cass. You're a fair person. And I know you wouldn't dis Felicia just because of stupid gossip."

"Or even just because of how Felicia dresses," Bryn added. "Because, as you guys know, we all needed some wardrobe assistance when we started the club." She tipped her head toward Cassidy. "You in particular, girlfriend, were not exactly what I'd call fashion forward, if you recall."

The others laughed, and Cassidy felt her cheeks grow warm as she started doubting herself again. Maybe she was wrong about Felicia. "Okay," she said quietly. "I'll try to gather as much information as I can before we meet." However, she had no idea how she was going to do this. What information?

"And I'll help," Devon promised.

"Great." Bryn's blue eyes twinkled with mischief. "I can't wait to hear what you girls dig up on poor Felicia. Sounds juicy."

"Bryn!" Emma glared at her. "I thought you *liked* Felicia." She looked from face to face with a disappointed scowl. "I thought you all liked her."

"I used to like her well enough," Cassidy admitted. "But I don't feel like I really know her anymore. It seems like she's changed."

"Well, I never knew Felicia before this year, but she doesn't seem like the kind of girl the DG needs." Devon sighed. "I know I don't say this much, but I actually like how you guys kinda raised the bar on this whole dating thing. I know I don't always act like it, but I appreciate that you have standards and morals. And as you obviously know, I kinda need that in my life."

"And I care about the DG." Abby stood up and reached for her bag. "My dad's not real thrilled with me dating in the first place, you know. The DG's my only hope. But not if it turns into something skanky. My dad would put the kibosh on that."

"That's true." Bryn nodded. "He would. I guess we need to remember we've created something pretty special here. We need to be careful to keep it that way." She smiled at Cassidy. "Thanks for making us slow down and really consider this."

"I gotta go," Abby said. "See you guys at 5:30."

Emma seemed to soften as Abby left. "Yeah, maybe you're right, Cass," she said quietly. "We don't want to do something we'll regret. As hard as it might be to pass on Felicia, it would be even harder to have to kick her out later on down the line."

"It could ruin the DG for everyone," Bryn said.

"Cass and I will get this figured out," Devon assured them. "And we'll bring the facts to everyone at 5:30."

"I'll tell Felicia to hang and that I'll talk to her later." Emma's mouth twisted to one side. "But I do hope you're wrong about her, Cass. I really hope Felicia can be part of the DG. I think she needs us."

Cassidy nodded as she bit into her apple. She didn't want to admit it, but she was feeling uneasy and wondering if Emma might be right. And Devon's talk about going out to gather "facts" didn't make her feel any better. How were they supposed to get facts when so far all Cassidy really had was a strong impression combined with what truly was only gossip? To pass judgment on Felicia based on such flimsy evidence—how fair was that?

Melody Carlson is the award-winning author of over two hundred books, including *The Jerk Magnet*, *The Best Friend*, *The Prom Queen*, *Double Take*, and the Diary of a Teenage Girl series. Melody recently received a *Romantic Times* Career Achievement Award in the inspirational market for her books. She and her husband live in central Oregon. For more information about Melody, visit her website at www.melodycarlson.com.